TO THE
MOUNTAIN
PEAK

Published under licence by The Self-Publishing Partnership Ltd, 10b Greenway Farm, Bath Rd, Wick, nr. Bath BS30 5RL

www.selfpublishingpartnership.co.uk

ISBN printed book: 978-1-83952-649-7
ISBN e-book: 978-1-83952-650-3

Cover design by Kevin Rylands
Internal design by Andrew Easton

Printed and bound in the UK

This book is printed on FSC® certified paper

TO THE
MOUNTAIN
PEAK

*Hearts open up in
moments where you
least expect*

IVAN KAGGWA

ACKNOWLEDGEMENTS

Without identifying everyone, mentioning some would be unfair. I wish to thank the many insightful people who supported and were a source of inspiration for this book, my anonymous whisperers, for their assistance and steadfast friendship.

Introduction

Growing up, I found out that life has a lot more to offer than just what the teachers in school moan about all the time, and I made it my mission to get it all, no not all, I made pleasure my target to explore and the best place to find that is our body. Our bodies are amusement parks and it's always up to us to know and learn which swing to jump on and which ride to take, but at the end of it all you must get onto something. Just like not everyone in the amusement park gets to have fun, when it comes to our bodies many just fail to know exactly where to find pleasure. Is it your lips, the neck, boobies, the round waist or the jewel diamond at the centre of your thighs? It has just got to be something.

While in school learning psychology felt stale, but when it came to Sigmund, I have never agreed with a thing like how I religiously connected to some of his ideas about sex and love. This geriatric fella made me feel good since I started exploring pleasure with my body at quite a young age. There is pleasure in sexuality which comes with erotic feelings and I am so comfortable saying that all our body parts can get to be erotic. Trust me, I have checked. Sexual appetite is every man's weakness, but at the same time it is a power, since it is a daily contributor to health and happiness; something that everyone needs and seeks.

The body has different features or parts on it, but I believe every part of the human body is erotic, and it can fully bring you the utmost pleasure, you must only find out how. Primary seven is when I found out about the pleasures that come with discovering newer things. Blood started running to the centre part of my body and in my naïve mind I had always wondered what comes after when my bulge is like a plant stem. It unsettled me most of the time, but it was one of those mornings when my mind got stuck on my first crush. She was dainty in my eyes and her little smile always broke my joints and stiffened my teenage muscles. I wanted her badly and the boner in my short pants always signalled my desires. As the sun rays started to peep through the rusty windows of my bedroom, it was more like a force I had so waited for just to slide my hands gently into my pyjamas. My mind was already set for this moment as the excitement was already building up and my heart was pumping so rapidly I knew that the general body part whom I call commander needed more fuelling. My hands were always cold but the moment they contacted the protruding bulge, it was all heat and satisfaction that followed. As I got to reach the centre of my pleasure just from a few sticky blows of a palm, it was a burst.

I have come to grow and appreciate sex and love because those are the two things that have given me the utmost pleasure, not money or any other thing. I learned to love through my early socialisation, with my parents, grandparents and a few people I met as I was growing up. These have been a clear guide on this road, and I carry that with me throughout my life. I guess that's why many of us look for partners that are a reflection of our parents; it is because they were our first teachers, and if they were bad at these two aspects it is more likely you will struggle to make it right.

When you get to find someone you love, you borrow their characteristics. Our brain absorbs their traits, ideologies, sentiments and attitudes so that we can form a connection that syncs and is hard to break. With all these in place, sexual desires and expressions also fall in place, and you let those bodies talk and feel and release all the pleasure and satisfaction it has got.

In this book I am going to share with you my journey from getting to know how fantasy is a principal in sexual excitement, how my body parts react to erotic feelings that get to overwhelm me, the different people that I have met in my life and how their different energies impacted on me, because trust me, each one came with horror, thriller, fiction and steamy action. Then there is this exquisite personality of a woman who am in love with. She shines and shimmers intensely, very elegant at sight, lips full of dripping honey, her voice sounding like a robin song, more like an electronic video game, her body shape is slender so my mind always instructs me to pin her to the wall and climb her to the peak. She makes me think of no other because she has made me extinct to others. I want to make love already. Anyway, it's time you walk with me and get to meet her.

CHAPTER ONE:
THE MAGIC TOUCH

In a rural side of the central part of the country, I found myself a devoted student in a school so dipped in religious settings and guidelines that I had no other worldly mission besides books, especially since at that time the idea of having a girlfriend would lead you into serious trouble. I was in my teens, and I was not about to be expelled or suspended just because my lacking ego was surrounded by female peers who were more like those flowers that are beautiful, dazzling brilliant and splendid. I just loved being around peers of the opposite sex because it's all that gave me power. I felt great being around them and my ego always cheered me up to it, seeing those smiley faces at every turn of my face made me roar because at least I had something to turn my mind to when on my skinny mattress in the night. I was that lonesome boy whose self-esteem was at its lowest, but I invested much of my energy in my looks as I made sure I was always dressed to kill and that my black school shoes were always shining. I was a bit raw-boned, with relatively ashy chocolate skin, but the best of all was the fact that I always made sure my perfume was on high volume, that is what made me a cynosure of all eyes. I always attracted the cutest belles just to come close for that good smell that defied the strength of sweetness. Hugs became my remedy because it became a norm that whoever came close enough wouldn't escape a wrap of my long, curvy arms, that firm hold that brings it all in while your body excitedly starts to command you to make it last a little bit longer. This made it difficult for me, since I always had on tight pants and in this case my body was never humble, it was an automatic tumescence, and the stiffness would make it worse for me to move around after those tight hugs. I always isolated myself in the corner so that my body would release me from the prison of sexual excitement. Damn, I was an amorous teenager.

High school didn't spare me from experiencing my first love, let's say puppy love, because all I can remember was having a hanging tongue when I was deep into it. As a boy who always got anxious just by having a girl sitting next to me, if I was to have any kind of oestrogen in my circles I just had to work on my confidence. I wanted it so bad, but I couldn't have it and that hurt me all the time, the need to experience love while you still can't hold yourself together. I remember it was one of those boring evening classes as we neared the close of the year. As I sat on my bench, head down, a soft warm hand lay on the back of my neck and a call for my conscience was made, wondering who was blessing me with a rise in my temperature by touching me softly. It was so feminine and smooth that I quickly rose my head and turned to see what God had sent me to redeem my dull evening. My right hand went straight searching for the hand on my neck and as I got a grip on it, I could feel that these were perfect long-fingered hands with a strong sense of slimness. There she was. Tamara, I said in doubt, and she replied, that's right. Suddenly, a charming smile covered my face, wondering at the miracle I had pulled to have such a beautiful soul appear to me. She wore a dazzling smile and sat right beside me. She was so calm and composed and her body was so swift as you could see by the way she waved it all around as if she was on the sea. Tamara had wide, ball eyes that were snow white and her face was long with full cheeks and a very refined nose, features that made her outstandingly gorgeous. Her lips were glossy as though they were dripping with sweet berry juice and when she spoke all I could hear were the melodious notes from her mouth. She was the true fantasy that could go on and on, but this time she was sat right beside me. I had never had a conversation with Tamara before and this was the first time she came this close to me. She came so close telling me about how she was just checking on me as a classmate and I was quick to appreciate her for her wonderful gesture, but deep down my heart was on a horse ride as my armpits by now were full of sweat and my temperature was skyrocketing. I got so anxious that my nerves started betraying me as I could see myself shaking, and at one time she noticed how uncomfortable I was and she came close and whispered to me that everything was fine, we could be friends. It was at that moment that I could feel her curved hips get in contact with my body, the feeling was soft, and I was set to be in the moment. I composed myself and I went light with a conversation. As she was getting up to leave she turned to me and she was like, would you mind a hug? I have never been so quick in my life to get up as I was at that moment, I was so geared for it and so ready to finish the day off with extreme excitement running through my body. I leaned forward and as she wrapped her hands around my neck, I reached out with my arms all going round those curves that were a perfect shape for my holding. I held her passionately and I told her goodnight with a bright face as if the sun had set on my forehead.

In the days that followed, I became so free with myself talking to Tamara and we would normally sit around in free time in class and just have open conversations. She was an intelligent girl who was perspicacious on lots of affairs of life, I learned from her as much as I connected with her. There was a planned trip coming up for geography and I remember us sitting close to each other on the bus throughout the shift. There were moments of talk, feelings and lust but more so my body always boiled by her being beside me. I wanted her and those moments where she could doze and just put her lightweight on my shoulders were the fountain of all emotions. I always positioned myself well so that I could feel her breath as well as sweaty skin on mine. It was a long trip, but the best out of it was the fact that I felt a connection with her. I believed her thoughts synced with mine, my feelings were undeniably on the plate for her to eat and our attitudes towards each other were so positive that it impacted my biological functioning, the thought of her was always a horse ride of my blood, and of course my bulge was always responding with hardness and pumps.

Tamara had taken my heart and all I could think of was her and how her gorgeous pretty face made my blood boil. Towards examination time I decided boldly to send her a card and express how I felt in the card, because it was the only way I could say it all. I wrote, "Hello Tamara, I want you to know that I can't live without you because you mean a lot to me. I love every bit about you and thinking of you makes me want to defy all the norms and just run to you every second of the day, you are special to me, and I love you. I wish you success in your exams." That was it, when I sent that card, I felt so powerful and I was so anxious and waiting on what was going to be the reply from her. I have never waited for something so impatiently as I did at this time. The next evening was the moment of reckoning, but gladly this came on a good note. I sat on my bed in the night after school time and my heart was blowing up, I didn't know if I was ready for what was in that card, but I had to put on a strong suit and flipped that card wide open, it was a card that had hearts over it, which was, of course, a good sign. She wrote, "Hello, Rain, thank you for your card and I just want to let you know that I love you and I hold you dear to my heart. Success in your upcoming exams." I have never felt how I felt then, because I am sure my adrenaline levels went through the roof as I started sweating rousingly. I was the man at that moment and all I could say was, "It's done." She was my first love and we had developed it to that slowly but intensely. My heart was excited, my lips were shimmering, my nose enlarged, my fingers became tingly as though I wanted to play the guitar, my legs were so restless, my stomach was boiling, but more interestingly my blood kept on concentrating around the bulge, she made me feel it all.

As the term was ending Tamara got sick with a slight fever and she was taken to the sick bay of the school for treatment by the school nurses. She was always surrounded by her friends during that time and all I could do was send in drinks and a few chocolates that I could afford so that she could get the care that I so wanted to give. I wanted her to be fine and yearned to see her, but going to the girl's side was never accepted by the nurses; boys had their resting area and girls also had their side. Days passed as she was recovering. I planned to cross to the girl's side just to see her. I asked one of her friends to be around the door just to alert me in case any nurse or teacher was to show up. I was so determined for this, I made my way to the girl's side and coincidently it was only Tamara in the room. She lay down on her back on a lower bed with her face looking up, putting on a welcoming shiny smile, she was happy to see me. I leaned down and hugged her tight as I whispered in her ears, "I'm glad you're getting better." I stayed sat beside her bed while holding her hand. I was on edge since I was in a place where I was not allowed to be at that time but had put all my trust in her friend. At least that gave me some confidence. After some time, I had to let her rest, but before I left my mind was already betraying me with a command that I had for a long time wanted to accomplish. I raised my right hand and moved it above her chest just to have a soft grip on her neck, my palms went all around her side neck and I leaned down to face her teary eyes. The more I got close, my eyes slightly closed and I put my lips gently onto hers, our lips were so compatible that they all got wet by how were kissing, I was so into it and my tongue went on to roll to hers and our breath started intensifying, my hand started moving from the neck downwards headed for those pointy breasts. It was at this point that we heard footsteps coming towards the room and my movement was so quick that I stood up within a minute just to give a distance; it was the friend showing up with advice that I should be going by now. If I was a fighter she would be wrestled – that was a moment she interrupted – anyway I had to put myself together and say my goodnights and goodbyes. I left that place but all I was thinking of was the moment we just shared, it was the first time we were sharing affection and it was a moment I was not ready to let go. My pants had expressed a tsunami as, by the feel of it, it got hard and then pumped and recreated and pumped and then released pre-semen, I had never had such a close encounter with affection, so my body was all up to the boil. I was hard the rest of the evening and my fantasies had grown into 3D since I could see everything.

We ended up doing our exams and ended school going our separate ways, but I did not forget to get those digits from her. I held onto her number like a precious ornament. We kept in touch almost every day and always did those long night calls that were so intense and full of wishes. Talking to her at this stage was magical because it was all I was having since she was not allowed to move to town under any circumstances, her parents were so strict that I thought of kidnapping her for a minute just to be with her and hold her into my arms. Our keeping in touch was so assuring and I was so looking forward to our future and getting into each other's arms again. Missing Tamara was more like that ongoing physical ache in my chest that always came with sadness, and at times it made me angry, I always lost focus and could not concentrate on anything and was thinking about her all the time. She got me badly.

During these times I was at the peak of my adolescence and always got hornlike projections. I used to move around the village just to get to see a girl or encounter a girl, that is all

I was looking for, I was more a cheetah in the jungle looking for prey but this time it was my sexual desires that had gone to the wild. At home, we were a middle-class family that had more like seven boys as siblings and we were relatively in the same age bracket. It is around that time that I was part of the few that connived in watching explicit videos and movies and always my pants would stretch as much from the stiffness of my machine, it was working. I devised means of finishing it off while watching these movies where I would position my rod between my thighs and just swing them continuously sat in one place until I felt my pressure getting above normal and my skin becoming sweaty. I could feel my boner getting so hard that it would pump in search of satisfaction and it is around this time that I would hold onto whatever was around and just feel a stream of fluid going through a pipe, oops, my pants are wet.

These were sex-tension times that required me to learn and know my body, since that is where all the changes were happening. At home we had rentals, and in these houses we happened to have a very glamorous lady, who could laugh at anything. She was so kind and caring but always was in high spirits. Her body was curvy with wide hips and a relatively tight waist, she always knew the value of having fun and on many occasions, she was the one that brought in those edgy movies that had put my whole body to shivers. This woman was so beautiful that all my brothers wanted to make their way into her pants and those round orange titties were ones to die for. I could envision having a suck on them, at least my mind finished the mission off. Tamara was always at the back of my mind, but my body was on a sprint of adventure, I just wanted to feel whatever there was to feel. I started getting close to this lady and at times I would sneak out from the main house just to go to the quarters and have conversations with her. She was relatively older, but we somehow got to have talks. One night, as we were at home, this lady came around and informed us that she was to relocate somewhere else and it was to happen in the next two days. I was disappointed just like the rest of my brothers but for me, it was pretty much because I had started liking her and she had noticed that because of how I was frequenting her house.

The day drew near, and she started packing her things bit by bit, but deep down it was aching that such beauty was no longer going to be around. Her voice was so soothing, and her smile was all so calming for me, it came with a high pitch that always caught my heart in a fist. Her last day at home came and, in the night, when she finished packing everything of hers, she called me gently into her house to say goodbye. I found her sat in a low chair and the only thing left for me to sit on was the bed, I sat calmly and I told her that I was going to miss her. She smiled at me and she said to me that everything would be all right, I had got attached to her and as she talked and smiled, I just kept on looking at her face, praising God how he had made this beautiful creation. She was a relatively short woman and whenever we hugged, she would fit around my torso area and just put her arms around my waist. On this specific occasion she looked up to my face as we exchanged this goodbye hug and softly asked me, "Do you want us to do it?" I stuttered with a confused face and said, "I don't know." I didn't know what to say at this point because at this point I was pretty naïve at how it all goes down. In my head there were just those movies and videos that I watched but the actual practice was on zero. I sat back on her bed facing down and I could feel her eyes looking at me, when I rose my head up, she was smiling, and she said I am going to miss you. It was at this point that my mind was very much sure of what I wanted at this point, I could hear myself saying, "Take it easy." The more our gaze met, we wanted to pounce on each other, and I remember she stood up and floated through the air like a lioness below dry hay grass as she was putting on a free short floral dress, she put her legs around my waist and sat on top of my lap facing straight into my face. At this moment I was so fired and all I wanted was to feel the pleasure in my arms. She leaned forward and started to feel my lower lip with her tongue as if she was licking honey, and at that moment I stretched both arms and pulled her ass cheeks apart and drew her towards my body more. My tongue started to suck on hers and as I intermittently devour her with my eyes. My arms held that round ass so firmly and at that moment I put my hands under her dress, all I could feel was bare skin, so smooth and warm. I moved my right arm to the waist as the left was glued to where it had started. The lips exchanged fountains of honey with each other and my body at this moment was at the highest of heights, my short parts had a hill and my phallus at this moment was more like a hungry lion. My arms moved up and I landed on these round nipples that were all hard and sharp. My fingers started feeling them all around and as I was doing that she started to breathe intensely and it is at this time I knew I was doing the right thing. I could feel her strong breath on my skin and as she held on to me, I could feel her moving her waist in a circular motion and pressing on to my hard cock in my pants.

As she was still on top of me, I removed her dress and looked into her eyes and asked her ignorantly, "Should I kiss your nipples?" and she answered, "Do it." I bent her back so that I could get some space and it was then I looked down at this body all on me foxy and delicate, but that was not the point, I could see my pants with a wet patch and it was not me bursting already, but rather her fanny was crying out loud, it was dripping all the oils that I had not seen with my eyes. I kept my left hand holding on around the waist and my lips went straight to those hard nipples and started to suck on them so gently, and at one moment I would bring out my tongue and started to feel both nipples with it and get to bite on them gently smooth. That made her wild and so got her creamier and dripping. I moved my right hand, sliding on her chubby thighs, and went swiftly onto the top of her fanny, it was so warm and as I started to flick my fingers on top of it. She grabbed me tighter and her moans intensified at this moment something that made me want to just unzip my pants and let her slide down, but I never touched my zip. I kept on rubbing her clit so intensely and slowly put my middle finger into the pot of oil. As it went down her moans became louder, and her fanny warmer and creamer. At this moment my bulge was pumping all in search of an escape and I didn't see myself holding on any longer. All I wanted was to put her legs apart and put it all in that soaked slit. It was at this moment that I switched her around and put her to the bed and I looked down on her while I was holding onto her legs. The view I had at this time was worth all worldly pleasure and at this time no body mattered, yap, even Tamara. But as they say, "When ill luck begins, it does not come in sprinkles, but in showers." I have never heard a hard knock like the one I had on that day, just when I was about to dip it in. It was my elder brother knocking on the door, persistently calling out for me as it was getting late, and they needed to close the main house. I have hated that man since then, I don't know if what he did can be forgiven, because that was the time all my excitement was going to be of worth, but a motherfucker showed up and I left a naked belle wet on the bed all aroused and ready for a romp. It never happened and I am still pissed thinking about it.

I left for my bed and all I could think of were the moans in that room as my finger was rubbing the prize and as it slid up, it was a long night of stiffness, but the sun saved me with its sharp rays. It was already morning and I had slept

TO THE MOUNTAIN PEAK

with a programme, so I ran very early to town and did what I had to do. When I arrived home, I was so broken when my eyes ran to open vacant quarters. She had left, and I didn't get a chance to say goodbye one last time. I tried to ask around, but she had not left any messages or told anyone where she was relocating to. My heart got so heavy, and it was all that feeling of unfinished business but more, so I had got attached to this lady even though we were nothing like the same. She was a fulfilment of my sexual desires at that time and I needed more of it. I tried calling but nothing was coming from the other end of the phone, she was gone, and I was back to those night calls with Tamara where all they provided was fantasy and hope. Hope that one day Tamara and I would get to experience as much pleasure as my desires suggested.

However, I was frustrated at that moment with being lacking. I never gave up on keeping in touch with Tamara: she was my high school darling, and no one was to tamper with that, at least until we get to the deep end. Towards the end of the holiday, I was fortunate enough to get a call from Tamara and she was all excitedly announcing that she would be in town tomorrow afternoon. I was happy to learn about her coming around. The day came and we met at an ice cream shop. She was as bright as always and still gorgeous as she has always floated on this earth. We exchanged hugs and we were so happy to see each other, but the tight part was that she came with someone, who was more like a drone above her head. Her time was limited, and she was not to go to any other place, so we stayed put and had some good conversations. We all showed how we were excited for college, where we would be freer as we were both going to be moving into hostels. We had a positive feeling about the future, and I was all ready to have some free time and get to share some freedom without being on the wings of anyone. Our afternoon was calm and good, and we separated with grinning faces because it had been a long time since we saw each other. We were just ready for college. Much as I felt love and so much into Tamara, I never got a thought of ever telling her of what had happened between me and a lady in our quarters. I just didn't think that was something she would want to hear. I condemned myself, but the comforting thing to me was that I was in a space of learning and exploring. I was too naïve to reason at that point. I just don't remember ever mentioning a thing about that experience.

Time moved so fast and the moment we had all been waiting for arrived swiftly, we were going to have our rooms and stay in hostels with no restrictions or boundaries to what we had for each other. Tamara ended up getting a shared room at a girl's hostel, which of course came with its restrictions, as visiting hours were limited to 21:00 hrs for men, and it was by no chance allowed for males to sleep over. All that this hostel had to offer were day visits, and praying that roommates were not loners who kept to the room always. As for me, I ended up in an open hostel that took in both men and women and my room was shared with one roommate; he was a fair guy who was a bit reserved to himself and spent most of the time playing video games. That was an automatic problem for me: this guy needed to have a life. Here we were, two young adults who had just joined higher education ready to take on the world but also explore what life has in stock for us. I settled very well in my hostel and put my timetable in check and was all ready to do the knowledge accumulation. Tamara ended up majoring in social sciences and my grades put me into psychology, a subject that I hoped would give me power. At this moment, as I sat in my hostel room, I realised that no matter the stage of your life, there are things as human beings we must experience; to some they can come early, and others may be late in life, but eventually you get to feel it. Adolescence is one of those stages and this comes with sexual excitement, we experience an increase in muscle tension, man will experience their testicles swelling and women will get to experience vaginal lubrication, this is part of us and as we grow, we get to have control and enjoy this excitement more and more.

CHAPTER TWO:
THE BRINK OF ORGASM

The semester of the year started, and everything was moving swiftly and promising, Tamara and I got to have some moments out and had different dinners taken, but all these dates were more eat-outs and then back to the hostel. There was not much time where we were just the two of us. In her room there was that tall lanky girl of a roommate always sat on her bed with her eyes glued on her phone. Tamara kept campaigning about how good of a roommate she was, but to me she was the barrier to my deflowering. In my room, there was this video game addict who went further and started bringing friends just to play games. Most times I would come around with Tamara from having lunch or dinner and boom, we find a swarm of video minions playing FIFA, I wanted to strangle them at one point but God was on their side since he created me nonviolent. They were just junk asses blocking my success to life, at least at that time.

I had a cousin at the same college and he was very into

the nightlife, I had never been to clubs or night carnivals but this time he came on a mission and told me, "Bro, you have to come with me this time, and you are bringing Tamara with you." That was exciting and convincing enough, so I called Tamara on this Friday evening and I was like, get ready to party. It was happening, both simple and green, we were ready to explore the life that we were so far from, but this time we had a guide that was a loudmouth and artful character, fit for the craziness of the nights in the city. My cousin came around 8 pm to pick me up and when I emerged from the hostel, my eyes went straight to a ramshackle Toyota car that was parked right at the entrance. His friend was driving and immediately my worry went to the car that was meant to be our ark for the night. It was in a very sorry state, but because having a car always came as exceptional to nightlife, I had to humble myself since I didn't even possess a bicycle to ferry my Tamara. I braced up and off we went to pick my girl up from her hostel, we parked in front of the hostel gate and I called her to find us outside. We waited for close to half an hour and then a light appeared, yes, she was light, and the rest all went into total darkness, just like how they do it in operas or theatres where the character at that moment is the only one in the spotlight. I had never seen Tamara in a skimpy short dress. This was my moment, my eyes protruded from their sockets and my mouth started salivating. She had put on this brown dress that had silver glittery lines. She was so glamorous and as she walked towards the car it was more like how Priyanka Chopra walked down that stage to be crowned Miss India, legs crossing in a catwalk. I was mesmerised and excited for I had never seen a dress fall on a body so perfectly. I walked out of the car and embraced her tightly with a hug. I then opened the back door for her to sit as I followed closely. Off we went for the night hunt of pleasure.

The night kicked off with a dinner at an outdoor restaurant and since I had never been to this end of the city, things were going to be very dodge since everything was against my wallet, it just did not agree. I'm one of those guys who always opens my wallet just to remind myself of how much exactly I have before I embarrass myself. Regardless, we had something to eat and there was a pool table in the lounge of the restaurant. Tamara and I went over to the table and put in a game. Much as I love the game of pool, this case was different, I was fully focused on the beautiful legs my girlfriend had. She always put on long things and at this time, I was just seeing a new feature of her that I was dying to feel. It was tempting, but I did what all men do when they go out with a lady: composure. I was cool and interestingly Tamara had never played pool and at this moment I was ready to be the teacher, my chance to be behind that booty was already presenting itself. I got the cue and told her, "Come close to me." She walked in front of me and closer to my body facing the table. The lessons had started, and the excitement was already showing on my face. With the cue in her right arm, I put my hands around her round waist and told her to bend her upper body slightly and stretch her arm holding the cue with the other palm, making a curve for support and aim for the white ball. She stretched and hit and all I could see was a black rolling down into the hole. She was excited to have hit the balls and she turned to me passionately and hugged me so tight, I'm sure the government would have gotten overthrown and we would have missed it, since at that moment we were in our world, and I was loving it. I did not tell her though that potting the black ball at the start of the game was total BS, I let it slide.

We left that place and went to another spot, which was more of a night club, it was too loud with all kinds of belles, and I was loving it. My cousin embarked on his drinking ways and as for us, all we were comfortable with was mostly water and a few energy drinks. I was sitting on a high raised stool close to the bar side and Tamara came and stood right between my legs. We were having a good time and she turned, looking at my face, syncing with the rhythm of the music and her body just winding in a slow movement as though expressing emotions. I held her closer and I followed her movement tightly. Her pretty face was bright, and her eyes danced with amusement. Tamara leaned forward and exhaled exquisitely in my ear. She got so close that I could feel her body warmth straight through her dress to my skin. I got so turned on at that moment and all I told her was, "Your beauty is a real fire that burns," and I could hear her giggles in my ear. She was made for this night because her body was so rhythmic to the music, and I couldn't keep up, but my hands never stopped feeling the shape of her body. I pressed my hands on her well-shaped booty that was tight enough to be covered in my palms. I almost carried her up at this moment as the only thing I wanted to do was to pin her on my hook, it was ready to fish. My spongy lips at this time started to kiss her neck softly. I put my hot breath on her skin and after I started to feel that spot with the tip of my tongue, you could feel she was into it as she held me tighter. I left her neck and put my lips to her right cheek, and I started pecking it intermittently and raised my hands to her waist. I just wanted her at that moment and didn't care who was around to defy the motion. I stretched my head up and like a spartan claiming victory I put my lips on to her lips and felt each so passionately. I kept on softly biting on her lower lip as though I was taking a red berry dipped in chocolate syrup. The night was complete for me with this feeling as an epitome, and I was ready to carry my trophy back to a warm cosy abode. It was close to 2 am and I alerted my cousin of our intentions to leave, we just wanted to go find comfort and continue this boiling intensity.

My cousin's friend gave us the car keys and they were hanging behind a little as the plan was that they would find us in the car in the next thirty minutes. We walked out of the club hand in hand and praised how well the night rolled. When we reached the car, we settled in the back seats and

I said, "I should get you home soon." I leaned between the front seats and put the ignition on because I wanted her to feel comfortable and be warm enough, but as I went back to my seat, she reached over and turned the ignition off. In her eyes, I could see that flair that was more like telling me, "You started this and so you're going to finish it." I was like, "What the f …" and before I could finish the sentence, her lips were on mine. We took soft breaths between kisses, getting deep and deeper into each other's mouths. I slid back in the seat and the only pauses between our kisses were when I took my t-shirt off and adjusted my position to get closer, I rubbed my hands up her waist under her short dress, eager to take her clothes off. She lifted her arms to allow me to take the dress off and from there I started to kiss her neck and collarbone slowly as I undid her bra. I took it off, fully exposing her top half to me. This made me look like a kid in a candy store. I trailed my tongue down her nipples and I heard Tamara gasping at the sudden sensitivity. I chuckled at her and continued to kiss down her body until I got to her naval, where I put my tongue deep in the curve and she could move swiftly and stretch in response to the tickles that came from my tongue sweep. I gently went further down until I reached her pants, where I turned the inner thighs and put my lips and them in bits, making sure my lips touched all that soft skin. All I could hear at this moment was Tamara's breath and how it was turning me on like a bull ready to mate. We had no regard for where we had parked at this moment, or if my cousin and friend would show up like party poopers, but all that didn't matter. At that moment I was sure today was the day when we would both get deflowered since none of us had been involved in actual fucking. From kissing and feeling Tamara's thighs I gently lowered my head and positioned it right between her thighs, I started to lick smoothly on the sides of her slit and I could feel she was already moist. At this moment while I was bringing down my left hand to pull aside the pants so that I could have a full plate for my serving, her thighs started trembling and tightened, something which signalled discomfort. At this moment, I put my head up and looked forward, asking, "Are you okay?" She replied in a broken voice, "I'm fine but am just not comfortable." I put on a calm understanding face and got up but deep down I was like, "What the fuck." She was stabbing my heart and of course my horniness. I was disappointed and didn't want to push it, I rose to adjust my pants properly, which had developed a hill already. I gave her the dress to put on and all I did was hold her so tight at that moment.

After some quiet time, my cousin and friend came around drunk but awake enough to take us home, I didn't have a licence at that time but if I had, there is no way we would allow a wasted guy to drive us back home. It was not responsible but we had no option and at this time we were just quiet to everything that was happening, just holding each other tight and embracing all through. We set off and at around 2:45 am in the night I knew my roommate was already salivating his mattress and fuming his gases in the atmosphere. My place was not an option at that time so we had to take Tamara first and my hope was if it was okay at her place, I would sneak into her hostel and spend the rest of the night there. When we reached her hostel, the gate was closed and so we had to sound the horn to see if the gatekeeper was around somewhere. He emerged out of the darkness, very angry as though we had interrupted a very important dress. But what else does a man dress about in the cold if it's not a woman? Anyway he opened the gate, and we made our way to the compound. I unlatched the back door, and we came out with Tamara a bit shaken, she was over with the night and the only thing left was her keeping her arms around my neck and her face resting on my chest. There was no way I could cross from the compound to her room, as the gatekeeper kept gazing in our direction wondering when we were to tell him to open that gate again. It is at this moment I remember telling Tamara, "I love you," and all she did was look up and gave me a light kiss on my lips and said, "Goodnight, baby." She unwrapped her hands off me and gently strolled through the compound slowly to the opposite ground balcony so that she could see us off. The night was awesome and as I sat back in that car I was filled with love and bliss as I got close to what life is about. The car was started and as it shifted from its position, the ignition went off and all we saw was smoke coming out of the bonnet, it was funny but at the same time rattled. This car was more like an experiment because the next thing I saw was my cousin's friend jumping out with a big spanner, and he was like, "Calm down." When I turned to the balcony Tamara was right there laughing, but interestingly the issue was fixed in a limited time, and we left the compound of the hostel swiftly. My cousin and his friend all came with me to my hostel room and spent the morning till it was sunny enough and sober as much for them to find their way. It was generally a good night for explorers like us.

We were happy people in our early days at college and all we did was find anything that we could try out just for the sake of experience. I was still that young boy who was just eager to learn anything from anyone and most of the time I found myself with different kinds of people just doing random things like visiting different hostels on campus or even trying out new foods in different corners of town. Tamara had her clique of friends whom she had progressed with from high school and these girls always moved together like a pride, it was always intimidating but that's how they had designed their lifestyle. I always met Tamara on campus with her pals and we just had a few moments to share. It was always fun but quick. At my hostel, I made a few friends, especially those that my roommate played games with, and spent most of the time in my room when I was off campus, and it's on a few occasions that I got to be in Tamara's room. It was always with her roommate, which was okay at this moment. I was on a path of life that was being blown by wind like a boat on an ocean. What makes life are the moments in time, that's what we get to hold on to, and for each day that I got to live, I was always blessed and thankful for whatever I found myself doing on a specific day.

My hostel was a big one with lots of good people, but the best part came unanticipated. It was practically a mild and pleasant afternoon until my stomach started growling. I was so hungry that I could eat a scabby horse or a blue whale if presented. Stuck in my room I wondered what to do at that time that could solve my hunger issue. My roommate was yawning as much with nothing to chew. Generally, we were broke boys. I had to go out and look for something to eat at this moment and as I was striding down past the ground floor of the hostel, my uncontrollable eye movement landed on this high and lofty gorgeous girl. I had seen her on my floor on several times, but I had never been this keen. Her smile was as cold and lovely as frost on a window plane. I stood still, just gazing, as she walked towards me all bright with her white teeth reflecting on her face. When she came close enough, she said, "You good?" and at this moment I still wonder where my answer came from, but I was like, "From which level in heaven did you descend?" I was so honest with my question because, for the time I had been on this block, nobody had ever bothered to know how I was or how I was doing. She laughed so loud that her laughter made me a bit worried, thinking maybe what I had said was silly, but she replied so tenderly after in a soft low tone, "I'm Keith." I told her my name and for a minute I forgot about my mission of solving my hunger. Keith had miraculously healed that for me by just giving me a portion of her time. At this point, I offered to help carry some of the groceries she had bought back to her room. She was so easy going and we seemed to be getting along with the way the conversation was going. On reaching her room she offered me a drink, which I accepted with no second thought, and coincidently she was preparing lunch which she insisted to share with me. In my mind, I was in a celebratory mood for the problem solved. I didn't have to move out again looking for food. She was the epitome of compassion and kindness, something that made me so comfortable around her. I kept on going to Keith's room on several occasions, and we spent most of the time watching movies and of course, food was always at the centre of it all, I was so smitten with Keith that any moment I had time on my hands was an opportunity to go to her room. At this moment, much as Keith was striking and an enticing force to survive, I had not made any advances at all because I still had Tamara in my streams of blood, even when we didn't spend much time together, she was still the one and I was just looking for that day she said, "Let's do it." From high school, there was no person I had fantasised about like Tamara and even to this moment I wanted us to share intimacy at any given moment, but she was not ready, forgetting that my rod got hard all the time at any given moment, making me ready. Always sucked.

The time moved and as we drew within a few days of Valentine's Day, I communicated with Tamara. She was free with no classes just like I was on the day, so I set out to go to her hostel. It was those days with a sunless sky, cold, quiet and so calm. I walked through the streets slowly but determined, just looking forward to seeing the one I called my love. I had a few notes in my cloth wallet and so I bought a tin of yoghurt and a tin of vanilla ice cream, which was her favourite. As I got closer to the hostel the smile on my face became wider and at this moment I couldn't wait to reach and just have a moment. I was in this mood because it was hard getting Tamara in her free time, so smiling to this call up was worthy. When I reached her room, I knocked three times and paused and after a few seconds. Her roommate opened the door wide with her handbag put in her armpits. She was leaving and to me that was a good sign. I smiled as we crossed paths and I closed that door firmly, Tamara emerged from the corner of the room in a purple silky night dress that I had gifted her when we were still in her school. It was the only material gift I had ever given her. She came close to me and hugged me so tight, and my hands rested on her slippery gown, I said to her, "It still fits." She smiled and raised her face and licked her lips and then with a stroke of her hand around my neck, she kissed me so delicately. It was a very beautiful kiss that till now I still want more of. We had a light meal that she had prepared, and she put on an adventure series to watch, *The Tudors*. The episode we were watching had more sex scenes than King Henry's complete sentences. It was a test of life and libido but at this moment I didn't know if I were to survive the dungeons because my pants were already uncomfortable and my eyes, all they could see was the brown, smooth, spotless thighs that were halfway covered by Tamara's night dress. I was strong but not strong enough to stop my hands from feeling them tenderly and gracefully. Tamara lay between my legs with her back resting on my chest and both our faces just glued to the TV.

At one point I started to kiss Tamara's neck and slightly sniffed on it as though I was a lion ready to suck the blood out of that vein. She was enjoying the moment of being in my arms and it is at this time that she turned her face and put her lips on mine. Her lips were so warm and soft and as we continued to press our moist lips onto each other, her lips parted slightly and gave my tongue room to slip inside, we rolled on our tongues passionately and my hands were already placed on those diamond nipples that hardened each time she breathed. I stopped calmly and looked at her pantingly and asked her an important question, "What do you do if you feel like you want it?" She laughed and told me an answer that I didn't predict at all. Tamara told me she had a clitoral vibrator; in my life, I had never seen one and I was curious. This was the perfect time for me to know how they work, since we both were in the moment.

Tamara got off the bed where we were sat and went straight to her wardrobe and searched deeply. Her hand emerged with a pistol-like gadget that had a handle and a hook fold with rubber bubbles on the edge. She came back in the same sitting position and spread her thighs and she put the vibrator in my hands and showed me the button, she said, "You turn it on from there for it to vibrate and press the second time to increase the spread of movement." I turned it on and moved it under her night dress, I slowly started scrolling down from the naval end and it is at this moment I understood that it was working because the moment it touched Tamara's body, her breath got wild and as I moved it down she started to moan softly as she relaxed her body on mine with thighs far apart. I finally got the vibrating end to the clitoris and as the vibration touched the spot, Tamara held on to my legs and her hips started winding in rotation, feeling every bit of that end. I was so tuned on that erection it felt like a sword in her back, her breath, her whirling, her loud moans and the way her mouth was open gasping for breath. Her titties were so big, and her nipples were ice cream cones just fit for my grabbing, I increased the spread of the vibrator and the more speed it had the more her pot dripped with honey ready for a lick, it was so soaked that my hands creamed from it. The moment came when both my hands were engaged around Tamara's inner thighs as she rivered from the source. At the peak of it all she took in the deepest breaths, loudest cries and shaking and all I heard was, "I'm cumming," and there she was all out all rolling onto my body. I was happy that I had experienced that but still, I was hard, and my problem had not been solved, I wanted to put it out, not with my hands this time but rather with service from another.

As she was there on me trying to regenerate, she slid her right hand on top of my pants and she realised the stiff man wanted some tampering with. She looked up into my eyes and as she kissed me intermittently her hand unbuttoned my trousers and made its way to whooper, it was a rock with curves of blood pipes stretched on top of the skin. I was feeling every kind of emotion right now and was breathing hot as though lava was flowing from my bloodstreams, the body was so hot and all I wanted was to erupt just right at the time when I couldn't hold it. Tamara got so comfortable that she stood up and pulled off my pants with her boobs swinging through that night dress and my rod at this time put upwards and strong as if it was a compass pointing north. She sat me on the edge of the bed and knelt between my legs and leaned forward for a better position, she put her right hand on my tower and slowly started to move her hand up and down slightly as she gazed calmly at me losing it. As she went on and on, I felt all my energy get centralised just in one point of my body that at this time was under full attention. She put her second hand onto it and started moving those hands in a rotation as though she was doing pottery. Her hands were so smooth and as she moved them, they became warmer and got sweaty, making my rod pump with excitement. I held on to the edge of the bed and it is at that moment that I heard drizzles of rainfall on the roof hostel giving a vibe that was much of intense. Tamara responded to this as if it was a signal of execution because immediately as it started drizzling, she moved her head down and put her lips on top of my cock. She kissed it and wrapped her lips around it as if it was a chocolate ice cream bar. It was a fire at that moment. She wet it with her mouth and kept on feeling the tip of it until she spat on it and opened her mouth so wide and took it in like a whale swallowing a boat. I had never got a better feeling, she gave me blows, moving her tongue all round moving from top to bottom and it all got soaked from her spit and I was boiling inside feeling all the pleasures that come with a wet weenie. At some moments she could try to swallow all of it and then pull it out. My pleasure raised so high, and my legs flinched, and a fire went through my body as my hands went straight holding her head to dictate the moment of those blows. I was reaching the pinnacle of pleasure. My mouth widened and my body got salty as I got to feel a rush of lightning coming through the pointed pipe. It is at this moment that I burst it all out on her tongue with a thick creamy load dropping in portions. My body was jerking and weakening but the pleasure was beyond and through to the top. She had finished me off.

That was the most bonding moment we had ever

experienced together, and this was an evening that had taken us to the moon and back and it was worth it on all accounts. I was smiling the brightest and as we both cooled off, I held Tamara to my body so tightly and we cuddled like grown cats in a cosy bed. As we were there in silence, I put my hand on Tamara's cheek and asked her, "Will you ever be ready for me to put all that package into your slit?" There was an awkward silence in the room but after some time she nodded her head and replied, "Let valentines be the day." I was so excited to hear that at that moment, especially since Valentine's Day was just a week away from this moment. That was a seal of white chocolate on the day that had been already awesome. We went out for a walk when night fell and strolled in those streets hand in hand like newlyweds. We were into each other, and nothing seemed strong enough to keep us from having the best of each other. We bought snacks for dinner and went back to her hostel, where we ate and watched one more episode of the series, but this time we were more focused on the TV than each other. I had to take my leave since visiting time at the hostel had clocked. Tamara walked out with me to the gate and gave me a warm hug and a smooth kiss on the cheek, which I willingly returned. It was a good evening at that moment with a bright night, even when it had started on a dull afternoon. I moved to my hostel the happiest man alive and don't remember seeing a person on the way since in my mind I was moving all alone in my space. Nobody mattered at that time. Just me reminiscing about my evening and looking forward to the pleasures that were yet to come in the nearby future. The coming days were so relaxed, and I don't remember going to any classes. All I did was stay in my room and play video games with my roommates and his legion of indolent buddies. Between that time, I didn't fail to get moments where I would just go into Keith's room. She was welcoming and that was to be utilised, for a person who has less pennies in the pocket and no glossary in the room. She was my go-to when my stomach needed refilling and when I needed a place to watch something quietly, but more so, she was the one with the brightest smile and mood. I loved being around her whenever I was at the hostel.

Days moved so fast, and the well-awaited day reached, Valentine's Day. This is a day that many who happen to be in love or have those they care for get to celebrate by showing affection through presents or gifts, cards, flowers and chocolates. Previously, this was a day I didn't put much emphasis on since it always came when I was at school or on holidays, times which didn't allow me to express my affection beyond a card or sending a note with a bar of chocolate to Tamara. This time it was different. Tamara called me early in the morning and had a plan laid out, she wanted us to have an evening dinner in a high-end restaurant and after get back to her hostel together. It sounded like a very good plan for the day and I understood she wanted that feeling of being treasured and treated as she deserved. Unfortunately,

I was not in a good place to actualise that. I was penniless as the wind, the only money I always got from my beloved mother just settled for my groceries. It was not much to have a balance to do such things as outings and all. I always stayed in my room or hostel because that was the choice that best fit me but if I had any more pennies to spend, of course, I would be out there more. I didn't want Tamara to know my situation and my ego played a role in that most of the time. As a man I can't stand not being able to do a thing. This time I had to lie, I told her my mum had sent me to go take care of some family business, which was going to take me a full day to accomplish. However, I made her understand that I would be back around 7 pm, which would allow me to just come straight to the hostel. She was fine with it, and she told me how she understood my situation.

Much as it was painful to lie, I was not willing to put my pride on a hook all in the name of honesty, I was so sure I got it all in control. I didn't shift an inch from my hostel and all I was counting were hours for me to get back from my made-up trip. As I sat in my room, my roommate showed up with three plastic rose flowers and told me he had got them from a Valentine's promotion going on at campus, I was shameless enough to request two because at that moment I thought of two people that I would gift them to. I was ready to take one to Tamara later in the evening and the other one would go to the person who had turned into my NGO with her delicious meals and friendship, Keith. Someone may think I was confused but if you are put in a situation where you wake up in a Ferrero chocolate company and all you must do is choose one flavour, I'm sure the contention would be between the black and white chocolate, they are all good, and that was the point when I was getting those two flowers. Later in the day, I sent my Valentine's Day text to Tamara, and it read, "Hello purple rain, we are here to experience this thing called life and I am so sure you're the only person that can make it seem heaven for me. I love you and I'll see you later, Happy Valentine's Day." It was that brief but pure and at that moment I didn't even care about the lie I made, looking at that text as consolation.

At around 5 pm as the day was getting louder with deliveries going to different rooms and streets full of cars and racing motorbikes, I picked one of the flowers and went to look for Keith. I found her standing on the balcony that was facing the road and on seeing me she smiled with surprise wondering whom the flower I had was going to. I told her that the rose belonged to her. It was a gesture from me for her friendship and for being a good person to me. She was happy and gave me a tight hug with a thank you peck on my cheek; she was filled with bliss, and it was so evident on her face. I was amused at how appreciative she was, even of a small thing like a plastic flower. While we were on the balcony at this moment, Keith was deep in conversation with me and I heard a ring on my phone. When I pulled it out, it was Tamara calling and at this time

I put the phone on silent and vibration, since I knew it was not yet the time of our meeting. Another call came in and this time I decided to pick up the call, all I heard was, "Why did you lie to me?" I acted in surprise and insisted that I didn't know what she was talking about. Tamara told me to look across the top curve of the road. It was a gloomy day, but what I remember seeing was a cackle of hyenas staring all straight in my direction through the tinted atmosphere. It was Tamara and her five friends; at this moment I was at a loss for words and softly I had to excuse myself from Keith, who was still standing close to me and moved across the road to explain myself. Tamara had seen me all this long on the balcony exchanging a flower and pecks with another girl. When I reached her space, I felt a quick sharp blow with her open right hand on my face, she appeared devastated and cross at this moment and all I had was a pale guilty face with the only sound out me being words echoing the "I'm sorry." She didn't give me a chance to explain myself but rather made sure that I knew and understood that she didn't want anything to do with me anymore, she was done. Her friends were more like soldiers guarding a general, they were protective and had faces that labelled me to be worthless at this point. They didn't like me a bit. I expressed how I still loved her with all my heart, but a lie had shuttered all the feelings of Tamara in just a few minutes. I have never seen someone decide on something so fast. It gave me an impression as though they were waiting for me to fuck up so that they could put me to condemnation. I was broken into pieces since I sincerely had a love for her since high school, but at the same time, I was not ready to put it out there that I lied just because I couldn't afford the evening she wanted to have. Still, my ego was not shaken, but as I come to think of it, maybe saying the truth may have turned things on a different path. She was taken away by her pals and I left heading back to my hostel with my head down in shame and uneasiness. I was more pressed and aching for an anticipated night going the complete opposite.

CHAPTER THREE :
THE CLIMAX

My day of valentines was not going as planned and at this moment there was no return from what had just happened. I was shuttered, and this is when all the flashbacks clicked of me and Tamara from way back when she first came to my desk and put her hand on my neck. She was my first love, and this is no wound that heals overnight, my heart still had a love for her, but this was far from what the future had in stock for me. The time with her brought me to realise how someone else can get to feel the same way you feel about them, she made me feel comfortable around her and other people because my journey with people was always associated with anxiety and shakes. She put me in a position where I believed she saw me in my entirety. This one time, everything was put to an end with a sharp slap and evil eyes from her friends gazing at me like laser beams. "They never liked me," I said, referring to her friends as I ambled back to the hostel. They always took her away from me and saw me as an incomplete boyfriend. They chose to ignore the journey that we had taken from when we were teenagers to this point and that was hurting to the bone. Seeing Tamara show me her back gave me an acute throbbing in my heart and my legs were weakened all through the walk to my room, it was near, but it seemed like it was the longest walk I had ever taken at that moment. As I neared the gate, I picked my phone out of my pocket to try reaching out to Tamara to get to put things straight, but when I opened it, I found a voicemail from her number. She was furiously at high-pitch volume emphasising how we were never to cross paths and how what we had was left in the past at this moment. To be honest, I didn't know this day meant a lot to her because in the past all we shared was petty stuff, and that made lying easy for me, thinking she would care as much since I was to show up that night, or the fact that she saw me with another girl on the balcony. I was just confused by the whole situation at this moment and all I was left to do was to find a spot and relax.

I went into my room and sat quietly on my bed looking so weary and pale. A friend of my roommate had already jumped into the space to start their trilogy of video gaming. At this moment I just needed a calm spot and all that came in my mind was to go home and spend the night away from all the noise. I packed my backpack with a few necessities and stormed out of that room because at that point I felt suffocated. On my way down through the corridors, my eyes landed on Keith and all I did was wave to her hurriedly, she was left with a confused face wondering what I was up to, moving so quickly like that. When I got to the streets, I tried calling Tamara again but this time I found my number blocked, I tried all through the journey going back home, but it was all in vain. I reached home miserable, putting on a gloomy face, and went straight to my room and sat gently on the bed. It was just me sat peacefully with an absence of motion or any kind of disturbance, but that was the switch that turned all my emotions at this point. I wept my eyes out and my face started flowing as water falls down the hill. I realised at this moment the actual feeling of loss. This was a new feeling for me, and it all seemed deeper than I had earlier taken it. I was hurting, and my senses were all reflecting that at this point. All soaked in sorrow I lay gently on my bed facing the ceiling and breathed in and out calmly trying to compose myself, and it was then that I heard bare footsteps walking in the hall and getting towards the bedroom. It was my elder brother Sam. He knelt next to my bed and leaned forward facing me. He raised his hand and put it on my shoulder and said, "Welcome to adulthood." He told me adulthood comes with pleasure, decision-making, purposefulness, experience, responsibility and loss. Those are things that move together through each person's life, and it was my turn to experience all of that. He was comforting and assuring at this moment because at this point all I needed was to know that everything is going to be all right. First love makes you think and look at your partner as the end of the road and them being the only one that can accept you, but in actual terms, you cannot predict much on how things will turn out in future. All you must do is try at that moment to make it right, but for this specific time I fucked up.

During my full week at home, I tried reaching out to Tamara for the first three days since it was then when the wound was completely open, but by the time I left for my hostel I was in the rebuilding mood. I was ready to focus more on what I could do better with myself at that time and what I could change with how I connected with people. One thing that I was so ready to work on was to be truthful to myself and others, however damning it may be or sound. It was my learning and my brother had done a good job showing me the truth about life and love, because it is a factor that we can't do away with. I was just not ready to feel as bad as I had felt in the last week, it was time to take the beast by its horns. I arrived at the hostel, and it was the usual atmosphere this time with students in all corners and school was just open for those ready to learn. I had not entered a class in the last seven days and my absence was not an issue to me since I was so confident that somehow, I would get help from one of the book warmers in my class that enjoy repeating a topic as many times to whoever feels like listening. Video games became my point of enjoyment as they put me in a spot where nothing mattered, and it was during these times that I gave a lot of time to games. I always spared time to go meet strangers in a pub and just play pool table for an evening, at one point I was very sure that I was addicted to the game since it occupied most of my time. It was just the only way I could keep moving without giving much attention to any bad feelings or energy that were deep in my heart. As time moved on, I was once again open to meeting new people and socialising in general, something that made my personality shift to a bit of maturity. Keith was a great part of my space because she was a young lady that always liked sitting on the balcony, and on many occasions I ended up sitting beside her and talking about random things. Keith liked going to the beach and at one time she got her phone and opened her photo gallery to me, it was full of gorgeous bikini photos that were so mesmerising to look at. In these photos she was in separate settings but the one thing that was not changing was what her spectacular body made me want. I stared on as I scrolled through what I could easily call a hidden treasure. I wanted to be in those moments but all I had now were the pictures.

One night, when the sky was lit with the sharp sparkling streetlights and the moon peeping through the white bright clouds, I heard a knock on my room, and it sounded powerless but consistent. I am that big head who is reluctant at everything and that included opening the door, but this time I stretched quickly as if I was expecting a paycheque to redeem my block life. I held onto the handle and swung it halfway to get a glance at who was seeking my attention. Standing aside from the door was Keith with her bright eyes rolling and wearing a calm smile. She invited me for dinner, and she was excited to inform me that she had prepared vegetable rice and beef curry, which are two things that electrify all my body organs. She didn't have to say it twice and off we went to her room. She dished the meal as I sat calmly in the chair waiting to taste the works of her magic hands. She always made delicious meals and I was sure this was in that same bracket. She handed out a plate to me and put the other in her right hand and sat on her bed and we started to eat, and believe me it was the ninth world wonder after Messi. I enjoyed the meal, and the non-alcoholic wine that she served with it complimented everything. I was at this point the satisfied crocodile that had no energy to lift my body even an inch from where I was sitting, I was thankful. I rested my back on the chair leaning backwards and we just spent almost an hour in a conversation about dragons and why they went extinct. Yes it was random but that was what Keith was more interested in. She made me realise that to get along with someone your mind must be ready to shift, adjust and be ready to learn, because at one point she made me feel like I was debating with her, and I was loving it. The night went on swiftly and there is no moment we thought of turning on that TV, we were so into talking to each other because it was flowing so freely. As we went on with the night we got to a point where we started complimenting each other and I was so willing to put to her how much a good person she was and from that I just targeted the features on her body and how they would move mountains because she was that outstanding. We reached a point of awkwardness and just stared at each other.

When she looked at me in the quiet, my stare moved from her teary white rolling eyes down to her well-curved lips, anticipating a word to jump out of her mouth, but since our thoughts materialised, the space between us was insignificant. I moved forward to the bed and at that moment, I just wrapped her in my arms as I positioned myself to fit on the side of the bed. We adjusted well to lying on this single bed that she had next to the side wall, it was so warm and affectionate. Keith turned slowly to face me, and I had no doubt about what I wanted to do. I kissed her lips, and they were so comfy to press on with mine. We both got into the mood and started to hold on to each other as we exchanged kisses deeply. I put a hand on her lower thigh, and I started to move it upwards as I exposed her inner area to more of my smearing palm. Our breath caught up with the pace of actions and her moans intensified as I continued to stroke her inner thighs with my hand and then further inside to her most sensitive area. At this moment we could barely lay in her bed, and I went on top of her and slowly spread her legs with both my hands and slid my right hand into her warm thighs. I put my thumb around the clit that was already moist at this point and I moved my thumb around it in a circular motion as I looked down at her face gasping for air and moaning so loudly. She was into the moment and so was I. I put my middle finger deep in her and her hips got so tight and she whined and I was gently moving it in and out intermittently. At this point, I was ready to dive my body into her and I just got up and unbelted my pants and put off my t-shirt, leaving me naked with whooper standing upright, it was at the same time she just slid off her short free dress from above her head. I got her down in a missionary position and put my finger back in her pussy and at this point it was dripping and ready for a slide. I fused my body into hers and parted her labia with the tip of the cock and then slipped inside the pot, it felt so warm and tight, and my thrusts started slower as I was kissing her and my hands feeling her medium boobs. My lips as I kept on dipping in would go to kiss her nipples and her hands were so wrapped around me that I could not escape, our temperatures were high and our skins were sweaty, but the friction made it all magic, the feeling of her labia holding my bulge firm in her vagina was heart racing. My thrusts got deeper and harder as she moaned at the top of her voice with disregard for her neighbours. I was at the greatest point of sensational feeling, and I could feel her thighs tightening on mine as I got deeper and harder. In that intensity, she creamed my whole piece while moaning with a high pitch of climax as if it was her last breath and it was right there when I shot a load inside her. Our juices mixed, and I felt her touching my face and telling me she loved me right before she passed out.

This was a moment of sensory awakening as I got to feel each part of my body react to this firing time of my life. Keith had just put me to the seventh heaven and as she lay down on her bed resting, my blood pressure was just through the roof reacting to the marathon of excitement that I had just completed. I was a happy man at this time, and I could see a future full of pleasure and adventure, my brain cells sparked and sent signals of love and it was evident by the look on my face that I was a happy man. Keith and I got to build a strong emotional connection and it gave me no chance to even think of my past at one time. I was a new reformed man with honesty and truthfulness at the centre of this build-up. We made a relationship that made everything easy, and I could visit my room occasionally just to pick my basic things but Keith's room at this moment was the nest. We got to a point where we would turn to each other for comfort, refuge and security and there was no room for loneliness or sadness, we just had each other. Keith was doing fairly okay financially, and I was not under pressure to always put something on the table because she had got it all figured, however, I also did go in hard whenever I got some upkeep from my mother. We spent most of the time together and did most of the things together, she was my light in the room and always gave me a smile on my face. While in this relationship, we came up with values that kept us bonded. We had awareness of the situation and if there was a problem it was always handled jointly, at any moment each one of us was free and open to communicating the issue, and lastly, we made it a point to always talk about our emotions and how we felt. Those were three things that this stage of my life handed to me as wisdom that helped to coexist and relate fully with a person. Keith was that girl that made me feel worthy and respected, and respect for men is love, no man feels loved if they don't get any respect from a woman, even when they are at their lowest or has nothing. There is a saying, rejection is entirely a result of your incompatibility and has absolutely nothing to do with your worth. My past was a mismatch because at this moment Keith and I were just syncing perfectly with the flow of life, living happily and most importantly fucking. Felt like the climax of life. We used to go out sometimes just to be with Keith's friends, who fortunately played actual snooker, and this was a foundation for socialising, I can't believe I made new friends, because I was not that guy. They always came up with activities in which we could always go and involve, and my best part was always the picnic and beach trips, any chance to see ladies in bikinis, and Keith always went above the bar with that because her body was a cinema in my eyes that I could watch anytime, any day.

As the academic year came to an end, Keith's friends arranged for a beach trip on the last Sunday of the term and were so hyped for it. I had some money in the bank at the time and I was quick to put our names for the trip, I just wanted us to have that moment and my girl was so ready for that party. It was always crazy with the guys. Many of them enjoyed emptying beer bottles and everyone knew this time it was going to be a run of chaos, but that's what made it fun always. The weekend was here, and it was Sunday already, which was highly awaited, it was a calm day with a bright sky ready to smear those skins with melanin. We stayed in the room for a good time as we waited for Keith's pals to gather at the front of the hostel, and after some time we heard a hard sharp horn, which was from a minibus signalling its arrival. Keith put on a long floral topless dress with cute simple sandals, and I had on my black shorts and white t-shirts with my ashy feet in slippers. We were ready to have fun and we went down the stairs holding each other's closest hand, a simple embrace to start the day with comfort. We reached the grounds and exchanged greetings with the rest and saw ourselves in the middle left-hand seats of the bus close to each other, and settled enough to not bother anyone. We just wanted to live in this moment just like the many we had made in the past. We set off quickly and the road was swift so that we arrived even without noticing throughout the journey that everyone was relatively quiet, and many were glued to their phones. From the entrance of the beach area, the music was booming through rusty speakers that were pinned right from the ground and they surrounded the area all through, the mood was set, and the evening was about to be full of "shake your bumper". Our feet were in the sand from the start, and we were all elated with the atmosphere and the breeze that was so soothing, the beach had palm trees scattered along and the place had different places that acted as platforms or eateries. We ate tilapia fish and chips as a group, which was more like a sundowner since at that time the sky appeared pink with beauty lining the edge of the heavens. It was so calm seeing the sun go to sleep with its reflections disappearing on the surface of the water, I turned to Keith and shared a kiss with her to seal the time. After eating, that's when the party was unlocked and unsurprisingly the group had more couples who turned to each other to counter the rhythm of the music being played, which was mostly dancehall and reggae. We were not any different, I'm not a good dancer on any given day but one thing I can't go wrong with is slow dance and the dubbing style where the lady gets to bend over. The music was on speed play and it put my energy in check, but I was down for it. I drew Keith to me as she was facing me and started to shake it like it was a competition, a high thigh protruded through her dress and stood firm between my legs as she wound that waist around and all I did was imitate her so that I don't get off key. It was energetic and beautiful. The best part of the dance was when she turned around to show me her back and bent, buckled and whined with her booty scratching on my upper pants, my lunch box was awakened at this moment. I held her from the waist and danced to her motion as I looked at her bare back. The Jamaican spirit took over and my dance became more hands-on. As she whined my hands felt her back and drew her to me with my right hand around her neck. She never stopped winding in her snake motion movement, and it was a turn-on for me.

The lights surrounding the area lit the place and I looked down at this unending strip of white sand meeting the clear turquoise waves. That was a call to go into the water for me. I asked Keith if she wanted to go into the water and she was down for the fun. She then stripped off her loose dress, revealing what she had on inside. She wore a tangerine seamless flowery bikini that accentuated her curves for every piece fitted in the right place, the bottom piece tied from the sides and the top one tied around her neck and back. It was a beauteous view, and it took me some seconds for my mind to align and function. I put my t-shirt off and bottoms and remained in my black boxers. We slowly padded towards the water hand in hand with wide smiles on our faces. The moment I felt water touch my feet drew me back as it was insanely cold, something that is no fun, but on the other hand, Keith was already kicking her feet through the calm waves and was pulling me right into the mess. I took my breath as I was being dragged but it was at that moment my mind reset and just put me in a safe position to just enjoy every bit of the night. I'm not a fan of water, being borderline hydrophobic, but in Keith's hands she made me risk it all and I was trying to swim as much as she was diving into the water. We didn't get to the deep side as the furthest we reached the water was stopping around our shoulders, something that made me look uneasy. Keith picked up on it and came closer to me and she wrapped her hands around my neck. I held her waist when she was close enough and we just got quiet at that moment, it was beautiful with stars looking down on us all in admiration of the pureness of the moment. We didn't mind what music was coming off the shores because the only sound we heard was from the water waves knocking on us and our breaths that were breaking from the coldness. Keith put her right arm on my cheek and said, "Whenever you come across water, always think of me." She knew my fears and this was one of the many she was helping me overcome it, and after that she brought her lips and rested them on mine. We started getting heated with affection as her kisses always made my body feel stoved, she gave me those teases where she could put her tongue out and brush it right on top of my lips. I would bring mine out and meet hers and just roll them together and get them deep into each other. My hands rested on her body but as we kissed, I grabbed her booty and just pressed it tight and we could feel the need we had for each other at this moment. We just wanted our bodies to go through each other. Keith withdrew from the spot and slowly paved through the water heading to the shores, I quietly followed her until she found a corner on the beach that had dimmed lights and put a light towel in the sand and lay on it as I squeezed on the sides for some space to sit. We weren't sure of where our friends were at this moment, but we knew when the time came to go, they would of course call, which gave us confidence in our isolation from them. As Keith lay peacefully, she started scratching her back as it was itchy and she asked me to massage on, she rolled over on her stomach and I started to rub her back with my bare hands. It was all going well and then I started getting lower, which prompted her to fold her hand backwards and untie the strings holding her top piece from the back. I continued to massage the back to the lower waist and seeing her like that was already turning my engines on. As I carried on, I moved my hands to the sides, brushing the sides of her breasts, and I could feel her raise her upper body a bit, which I took as a go-ahead for me to go all the way around those boobs. Already her nipples were so hard when my fingers went over them. I massaged her lower back, caressing the black birthmark just above her bikini bottom and my hands slipped a little bit under her suit as I continued to move down her feet. This had got into a full body rub. Without minding who we shared that beach with at that time, I rubbed her curves gently and turned to her exposed thighs and put my hands all around them as if I was smearing butter on a chicken. I was loving it and it was evident from how my boxers were stuffed at this point. I had a rock stretched out. While I put in the work with the task, Keith spread her legs slightly as I reached her inner thighs, which I gave a slow but firm treat of my soft sticky palms. My fingers skimmed against her vulva, and I could feel how wet it was through her suit, I slid my finger under her bikini bottom and gently touched her dripping slit. She turned around and lay on her back and beseeched me to finger her, but I teased and tickled her clit blandly, making her whimper. As I continued feeling the warmth of her flower, I laid down beside her and she turned her face towards me. I kissed her passionately, pulling her body close to me. I brought out my tongue as though I was reaching out for ice cream and sucked her bottom lip into my mouth, flicking my tongue against it. She was so glued to my body that she could feel how hard I was. She slid her hand down my body to grasp my hard cock, and I moved her hand away and whispered to her, "We are in public." She replied impatiently, "There is nobody around, no one is going to see us." I was not convinced, and I kept explaining but she shut me up with a kiss and she could feel me giving in because at this point I wanted it so much. She made another attempt and slid her hand into my boxers and ran her fingers up and down my hard whooper. I groaned and shoved my tongue deep into her mouth, as though I had been taken over. I rolled on top of her, spreading her legs and wrapping them around my waist with one hand on my chest and another still holding the bulge. She then put both her hands around my neck and with my cock slightly out it pressed against her pussy and our tongues danced in each other's mouth. The night was calm, and the waves drowned her moaning. We both wanted to make love to each other because a fire had passed through our bodies. I untied the string around her neck and threw aside the top, exposing her sharp boobs to me, and I covered her left nipple with my mouth while I was flicking it with my tongue. I fumbled with the side tie of her bottom bikini and fought until I untied it and then kneeled back and peeled it swiftly down off her body. I put my boxers away and it was two naked souls on the white sand. We were sucking each other's lips, it was all juicy and we were running out of breath with emotions covering every step of what we did. The moon and the stars made the night perfect. I sat with my legs curved and crossed from the front and Keith raised and came right to me and sat on top of my lap and I could feel her drip around her thighs. We got in a face-off position as her legs wrapped behind me. This position was so intense as we locked eyes and made our lips inseparable, my hands were exploring her boobs while kneading her nipples, and her moans were intense, and they drove me crazy. She passed her hand between our bodies and grabbed my bulge, which was slightly down, and positioned it to her slit and slowly sat on it, moving down half of its length as she moved her waist in a circular motion. She was wet, and I could feel both our parts getting extremely soaked. With her hands holding onto my body, in this position, she controlled the pace of the thrusts, she could whine as she moved up and down on that rod and she could sit on all of it, which always drove me nuts, she never stopped swinging herself on it and it made my rod pump inside her as I reached the edge of pleasure. She got a speed moderate, and it kept on increasing, making us moan in bass and soprano at the same time. We held onto each other as our bodies got salty and quaky and at a high frequency of friction, we were at the climax of it all. It was the big sigh of hard work of emotions. Keith rested her head on me as she gasped for a breath and slowly unplugged off me and crawled back to the waves.

Going back into the water was our point of refreshment and there was nothing that we felt for each other at this time that was not love. We had got into each other and had connected on a level that I had never experienced. Keith made me feel like I knew everything and could try everything and that was the magic behind my love for her. We had just experienced the best night and that was a memory to carry with me, she was that girl for me.

We collected ourselves and made it to mingle with others who were drunk when we got to them. They were having fun just as they should, and many were sat in couples just holding each other. We got a vacant table and sat quietly, but our faces showed the fatigue that we carried at that time. We just wanted to go back to our bed and hold each other through the night. Close to midnight, everyone was over it, which was the right time for all of us to retire. We boarded our shuttle and all through the journey we had fewer words for each other but more touches. We could not keep our hands from each other, we just wanted to embrace more and more. We reached the hostel, and we were comfortable spending the night in Keith's bed. It was a relatively small bed so holding each other was fitting, especially for warmth. We lay like heavy bags without repositioning with our bodies worn out from the day, but it didn't stop me from looking at how peaceful Keith's face looked. It was so beautiful with those eyes closed and all complacent with no sign of insecurity. The following days of the week were busy since we were finalising the year and everyone was just putting their things together. I packed my things and sealed them, since I was not sure if I was coming back to the same hostel for another year, or if fate would land me elsewhere depending on the financial stand at that time. Keith was so sure she was coming back and for her, it was just the essentials that she packed to take with her. The last day came when everyone was supposed to be out of the hostel and many of the occupants left in the morning hours. For me it reached 2 pm and still I had not got a perfect plan on how to get home. Keith saw that I was frustrated at this moment and when she was fetched, she was kind enough to go with me in her parent's car, since we were going the same direction. She was all out for me and at that point, I did not doubt if she was the one. Many times, in a relationship there are things you can consider that make up a healthy relationship; if you can communicate openly on anything going on in each other's lives then that gives you a ground to bond on and keep solid. There is an aspect of trust, which comes with honesty and integrity, that leaves no secrets between each other. A relationship with no secrets can stick together and fight for each other, which brings me to the factor of being able to rely on each other with mutual support from both directions. Being curious in a relationship is also fundamental, as this makes you interested in your partner's thoughts, goals and daily life, which eventually gives you a basis on how to support each other. The best way to support each other is through being teammates, since a relationship is more of a team that requires teamwork to achieve your desired targets and tasks or goals. Keith and I had put all this together and she had put that sense of maturity in me that was not all about physical intimacy, but rather many other things that were as important, and just as we prioritise time together, time apart is also healthy in a relationship as it gives you your personal space to have time on your own and get to do your hobbies, or just have a moment to relax by yourself, and a holiday at this time was a much need space for both of us.

Nicholas Sparks said, "The scary thing about distance is you don't know whether they'll miss you or forget you," and on my side, I was truly missing Keith, and this holiday was a thorn planted in my shoe. I was used to seeing her gorgeous face in the corridors every day or next to me when I was glued in her bed enjoying her warmth, much as she adored mine. Days were slow and nothing was fun during those times. We made it a habit to communicate, and those phone calls would be long and painful with floating desires and affection that were demanding more than just voices. Keith planned between the holiday for us to meet, which I was happy about and we indeed did meet up. Seeing each other was more of a moment of solace between two hankering souls. She picked me up from home in a blue comfortable Mercedes car, spicing the day up with class and style. We drove a short distance, got to the mall hand in hand and settled for a Mexican restaurant, since we both craved some tacos. It was a day moving on the right pace filled with smiles and love and we kept it less about words and more about gazing at each other with admiration, and the words we shared were often compliments. She was so glamorous and her face too bright with her white teeth sparkling every time she smiled. The evening was going so well, and I prayed for it to not end, but it reached 7 pm and we eventually had to go back to our respective residences. Keith requested I drive, which I was happy to do. We set off and reached my home, where I parked in the compound in front of the house. We didn't have a built fence around but rather what separated the compound from the road was merely a border of cherry laurel hedging plants. I put off the ignition and we went deep into random conversations with no sign of stopping, it was evident we had missed each other and if possible, we would go on and on just to have each other side by side. Keith wore a Victoria Beckham perfume which was damn strong and all I could interpret from that beautiful smell was to just embrace her in my arms. I repositioned, leaned forward in her direction, and held her in my arms, putting her on my wide chest with deep affection. She always got my nerves shaking since she had broken all my boundaries and she was everything I was insecure about. Too sweet, too kind, too understanding and too gentle, but most of all she was foxy. There is no way she could not sweep me off my feet every time I was in her space. Keith was also a teasing girl, and in that silence of embrace, she began with her tickles, putting her magic hands on my sensitive parts. If there is something that makes me jump out of my seat, it is tickling my waist and my ears, and she knew my reaction was always going to be wild, which she always found hilarious. Much as there is sensitivity in tickles, they excite me sexually, and at this point I was already in it. I didn't want her hands to stop and in that joking moment we gave each other kisses intermittently, she was starting to express the need to leave since time was moving, but we both didn't want the moment to cease. With the night getting cold and dark, it started drizzling and Keith relaxed in the black leather seat of the car with a casual smile on her face, making herself comfortable. She raised her left hand forward to me and started touching my shorts with her long fingernails scratching on top lightly and tracing the line of my bulge. It was getting a bit hot in those seats and the clothes now were becoming obstacles to the desires rising in us. We had our blood boiling and Keith teased open the buttons on the front of her skirt, exposing the skin beneath slightly. I was dying to see more of it and so she lifted the soft fabric down on her thighs, revealing part of the pink lace of her knickers covering her slit. I could not hold my hands, I just reached out to her inner thighs and put my fingers on top of her seabed, it was warm and crying for an embrace. I adjusted her seat and made it fairly flat backwards and gave her comfort as I parted through her vulva with my middle finger and went deep, making her howl as she cringed in the seat. We were suffocating in desire and as I carried on, I lamented the feeling, and in a minute she got up and pushed my seat backwards and pulled the plug, making it fall to the backside. She hurriedly unbuttoned my jeans and climbed on top of me and skimmed down on my already erected rod. She was moving her body voluptuously and she kept it in a steady motion as my arms held her bum so firm in rapture. She took me on a ride, and we exchanged wet kisses as her speed got more vigorous as she went all the way down on the bulge until we both reached a pinnacle. It was followed by exhaustion, but that just gave us a long motionless moment of just being stuck into each other. She stayed on top of me with her thighs adjusted around my lap and my hands just held her tight in the position. If it was possible, we would choose this moment to be endless, but she had to leave and get back to her home and I, unfortunately, could not invite her inside my parent's house knowing my brothers were probably already somewhere peeping with their eyes out to see whom I had come with. Keith put herself together and we both moved out of the car and hugged tightly, saying goodbye to each other. She sat back in the driver's seat and drove off. It was a beautiful day that we had shared, and that night was all peaceful and special and all that could show on my face, full of bliss. I entered the house and without interacting with anyone I sat on my bed with my phone in my hand. I didn't settle until I got a message from Keith informing me that she had reached safety. I slept the happiest man, and the remaining days of the holiday were all reliant on the fact that I would at least get to talk to Keith on phone or chat with her by text.

CHAPTER FOUR:
THE AFTERMATH:

As time went by, school commenced as it was the first semester of that academic year of study. Keith and I happened to experience a preposterous predicament where we resided in different hostels this time, which put our relationship to a test since it appeared as if an escarpment had gotten between us. It was those moments when everyone seemed immensely taken by studies and our meetings now only occurred once in a blue moon. We reached out to each other not as much as we used to. I tried to do that, which I thought was enough to sustain the bond we had, but as the saying goes, "Out of sight is out of mind." I can't quite place when the spark started to dim or when the distance between us was more expansive than from the capital city to my home village. Keith and I had created something special where we were querencia for each other, and that is what I thought made our love indelible. Our communication downturned in gradatim, however, we used to make all the efforts to meet up at times and with our smiles, on those occasions, we could sense the fear of being away from each and that kept us fighting the battle of emotions so that we could keep the flames burning. Keith used to come around my hostel most of the time where I resided with a roommate whose ebullience was contagious in a way that we could spend all time talking and laughing about random things. Unlike my previous roommate, this one had at least a personality which I could tolerate longer, especially since he got on with everyone. The only silly thing he ever did was one time I got ill with a fever, and I was having no one around. Him being a typical gawk and a complete ignoramus in this area, he got my phone and went through my contacts and ended up calling my ex-girlfriend Tamara. Much as the response was positive to the extent that she came and visited, I was so mad because he didn't have to do that and no one wants to be seen by their ex-girlfriend when they are down. It made me feel desperate with life, which was not the case. The term moved quickly, and, on some occasions, it was too slow to reach the next hour, especially in times when I was missing Keith and I could not get to her or she was not picking up her calls. Everything seemed incomplete and my heart was not ready for the ache of misery. Keith was my Schatz, and I could not bear the feeling of her being away, putting all the other factors on a scale I was missing the affection that we shared at any given chance we got while at her place. She was worth missing because of the things she did, and who she was, the way we entertained each other and saw importance in each other, and the way she always reminded me that I mattered.

On days when nothing was going on, me being a clinomania, especially in the mornings I lay down on my bed facing the ceiling just thinking of love and tapping deep into my feelings. It's understandable and fair to say I was in love, and I had gotten peace from a person that always flamed my heart with desire. In the evenings I used to go to the top floor of our building just to feed my opacarophile urge and it is all those moments that made me reminisce about the beautiful moments when I and Keith would just feel good by seeing the sunset, especially the beach moment that sealed our hearts. The term ended quickly, and we became more apart, even with the left strings in communication, the bond had scarred so badly to the extent that a day would go by without hearing from each other. We were no longer the hand-in-hand pair that could not breathe without each other, and Keith seemed to be more engaged in whatever she had going than what we had, even with things seeming to be shaky, I maintained equanimity with the hope that we would find a silver lining. Just like all other days start on this one day of the week, the morning was calm with my body pumped with energy, ready to encounter all tasks ahead, I received a call from one of Keith's friends, she said hello, sounding so low and confused and my instant reply to her was, "Are you okay?" She replied with generated effort and told me she was fine and after followed it all with a question directed to me, "Were you invited?" and with the confusion, I responded with a firm open answer, "Where?"

At this moment Keith's friend took countless breaths, wondering where to start from as she had called thinking I knew a thing about what she was bringing up. It is at this moment that I got to know that Keith was scheduled to marry someone else, and invitations were already out amongst her friends. This was a total blow in my gut as I didn't know how to get on with this news. All this seemed oxymoronic to me, knowing that I was still in a relationship with someone, so how would they be going for marriage with someone else? Her friend told me all this and my heart turned frigid, and I felt mediocre. Her friend's words on that call were innocuous but informative, since they found me in a state of ignorance on the matter and I had to take the tenacity of making the most significant call that mattered more at that time. It was perplexing, though, that Keith's friend, whom I first saw on the day we were at the beach, which was the first and last time we met, took the initiative of looking for my number to tell me this, not that we were friends, I guess some people are just silent antagonists. My heart was burning, and I started adding up things, thinking all this poor communication that had progressed was merely an augury leading me to this moment. I called Keith to get her side of this rumour and the first two calls were not picked but the third one out of persistence was picked and you could feel she had hesitance in her response, already thinking about what I wanted to ask because my first words on the call were, "Is it true?" and her reply was as plain as, "About." She didn't break the ice until I was open with her asking if she was indeed getting married, it was close to a minute on phone with no word coming until with she spoke with the deepness of her voice saying yes. My knees got weak and my body got a rash covering my skin, I could not believe it and words left me because I couldn't find the right words to put out at that moment. Keith told me she had known the man she was going to marry from way back, since they were close to her family and they had been matched by both families, and that is how it was meant to be, and in a shaky, disgruntled voice, I asked her "What about us?" I wanted to know if all we shared meant nothing to her but she was adamant to explain at this moment and it is then that I learned that Keith had made me redundant.

I request to meet Keith while she was still on the phone, and she was fine to come around to any place just to tell it to me straight. We agreed to meet in a lovely restaurant surrounded by trees, which I was sure could create the serenity that I need at this moment. Keith showed up with a composed face and I was in a calm mood to share a hug with her because all I wanted to know was if all we shared was just a passage through the road or her selling me a mirage character. The sunlight shined through the tree leaves straight into our faces as though it was a torch lighting up the dark with nowhere to hide. I just wanted to hear what she had to say, and I was ready to accept it in whichever form it came, though at this moment I was wishing for the story to change. Unfortunately, she confirmed everything to me about how she was going to get married under a family arrangement and she had no control over it since it was something she had learned of since way back and they were in courtship even when the gentleman was not living in the country. So it all seemed like when her main man came back, I was ready to be put to the ditches. I felt like I had been hoodwinked into what I thought was a perfect love story. I was so dejected that veins showed up on the sides of my forehead, which look like a road map to Scotland, I know that's extreme but yes, I can't make that up, when you looked at me at the time you could just be directed to Edinburgh. Keith showed no sign of sorrow or remorse on her face, which I believe was an indication that she had thought through all this in the time we were all apart with less connection, that time was enough for her to break and rebuild, although on this occasion it was me being broken. All I took on that table was a glass of water, which I believe was extinguishing my burning heart at that moment, but all the heat could show from how I was perspiring. I was hurt and I could not stand the feelings that were still exploding all over me for this beautiful girl, she had got me good and treated me to the sweetest of cherries that I could fathom her being elsewhere and not having her in my arms again. Sadly, it was happening, and in a quip way, Keith asked me if I wanted to go to the wedding and I remember giving her a very humble reply, "Fuck you." I was just murky right now and jokes were the last thing I could take right now, that's if she was joking but that was more of a close to our meeting and in the next few minutes, she stood with her hands spread ready for a hug. A hug is not something I would do in such instances, but I did stand up and held her tight without wanting to let go, it was goodbye to us, and it was not a nice feeling, but all I did was cherish the ephemeral moment that we had shared between us. We both left the spot at the same time and went in different directions, but the ache I had in my body was nebulous because I couldn't understand what I was going through, which was more like a cocktail of emotions. As the wedding day neared, I stayed most of my days at home trying to survive the reality of life and one day, as I walked around the village, I crossed paths with a coot who echoed all kinds of words to whoever dared to listen and this time one sentence settled deep to my heart, "There is more to life." It may seem plain but at that time it was enough to lift my mood, which I had dragged down since that meeting with Keith. My days were obscure and nothing was going on in my life since I had not gotten a job at this time.

Much as I aimed to elude from all to do with Keith on her wedding day, the era of social media gives no room for that. I'm not a resentful person who deletes, unfollows, or even blocks someone when we separate, but that proved to be a problem since Keith's wedding celebrations and events were all over her accounts, or at least someone on the wedding was tagging her. It was a day of agony for me, and I carried that weight all through the day since I kept opening to see videos, pictures and slides, showing how happy she was. She was gorgeous in that gown, it was just disheartening it was not me beside her. This dilemma in my life made me feel levitations as I could not comprehend what exactly I missed. Sometimes things happen in our life that are unmanageable and all we must do is just carry on and see where we land the next day, life never stops until you breathe your last and until then, we wake up and keep moving. I knew it was not going to be a simple walk through the light, but I was ready to take it even when I knew Keith and all that we shared was going to be part of me for some good time. She was good but her best was not preserved for me, she was gorgeous but not for my keeping, she was sexy but all that was for another person's enjoyment, she was charming, but all the giggles were to be directed away from my face. She was not mine to have, even when we shared moments between us. She settled for someone elsewhere and it was up to me to do the same rather than keep whining. Being alone most of the time helped give me insight into what to do with my life again as I started to do some good charity work that dealt with sensitisation of the population about HIV/AIDS. This was my gateway to being out there and I was enjoying meeting new people almost on daily basis, these people shared stories about their lives and made me feel like I had a greater purpose, which I could fulfil right where I was. I travelled in different areas with a team of youth just talking about the significance of minding your life and how best to protect it when involved with other people.

During this time, I was fortunate to be out there and socialise with different kinds of people and I was able to make friends who gave me beautiful moments that brought out sides of myself that I didn't know I had. It was a time of self-awakening and self-realisation, since I got to know what am good at and what doesn't fit well with me. In the evenings after fieldwork or trips in those rural villages, we used to go out and just hang around with the locals. Playing pool table for me was always enough because that was the only thing that gave me total excitement when out there. Most of the pals I had around were boozers who could empty barrels for fun in the night but the only time I tried to swing a bottle all hell went loose as I almost lost my intestine in vomit, I just gave up on that forever. I was taking steps of courage in the right direction, and it made me ready to go to whatever place my heart was to point at. I didn't know where but I felt content and steady for a perfect landing. I was finding myself in places I had never imagined and I was speaking words to the people who were ready to listen because they needed them, I found my strength in the words I spoke and throughout this time of sensitisation under the NGO I started conducting therapeutic talks to couples that always came in our teaching seminars and while I was talking to these strangers, I got to recuperate and remove my heart from the trenches of misery. It had been a long time, but in those talks all made sense to me and I realised that the true meaning of life is what you do in it and how you live it. I met young beautiful ladies in this programme, and it was always refreshing mingling and going out on dates but in most cases, things didn't seem to work out since in most cases it was lust that I carried, and my desires normally vanished after one-night stands encounters with a few of my peers and some that I met on the programme in the places that we moved to. Being in different places on the programme was always fun but the most unforgettable moment that I cracked about to date was when I went to book a room at a local lodge and the receptionist was kind enough to inform me that I should wait for thirty minutes, since someone had to go in with a prostitute for a short service. I laughed in amusement and asked if she was seriously considering giving me that same room, she was so sure with her yes. I couldn't take that room and it was only that day that I chose to sleep in a company car, I was not ready to smell the odour of someone else's enjoyment.

I carried on with my activities and luckily enough during this period I got to do a part-time job in photography, which I loved so much, one of the many reasons I loved it was having glamorous ladies in the studio and capturing their poses, it was a quench to my thirst. I used to talk to a few of my friends from high school and I was able to land a few Kairos that made me connect with them on a friend level. I was getting hired to take their birthday pictures or even pictures on normal general gatherings. One day I was contacted by a group of girls from among my OGs who wanted to travel with me to the east of the country and take photos of them while on their adventures, luckily enough I was friends with most of them, even when we didn't often communicate. It was an easy decision for me to make and the add-on was the fact that I also enjoyed going on trips. It was a trip of two days, and it was only me in a group of five girls. They were all jolly girls that were full of life and their beauty was not something to challenge all the five. There was one that was magnificent and exceptional, and she was easy to point out from the many as she was the talkative one. She was the one that had contacted me for the job and her name was Charlotte. We had crossed paths during high school time, but we didn't get to share any lengthy conversations then since I was marked for someone else at the time and no one would even stand close enough, otherwise she would have felt the wrath of those that thought they owned me. On the day of the trip, I gazed at Charlotte; she was so effervescent, succulent, charming and beautifully curvy that I was swept off my feet, and when she approached me with her striking smile, I was already sure of my next step. On our way to the destination, I sat next to her and her eunoia made me see her as my mark of reawakening. Her charm was something that made me attracted to her. Nicholas Sparks was wise to say that "the emotion that breaks the heart is sometimes the very one that heals it." I was right at that point of excitement, and I was ready to express it all through. The journey to the place where we were going to spend the night was interesting and it was filled with stopovers for refreshments and dining since it was a long journey but, on my side, at this moment I was just fulfilled by the fact that I had the right person sitting next to me. At one time while on the bus I looked at Charlotte and she was close to dozing when she was awakened by a hump. She turned and I was right there looking at her all this time. All I did was compliment her, told her she was the face of the sun, and she burst in laughter, though to me I was sure she was by the way she lit my heart.

The girls had planned to go to the river and go around seeing some wild animals and after a long drive of about five hours we arrived at the national park, and the immediate task we had to do was to find a hotel where we would spend the two nights. It was an expensive area, and the goal was to at least try to get something cheaper that would accommodate all of us. The problem came from how many rooms we were to get and since we were six in total, we settled for two rooms with two bedrooms each, the four girls were happily sharing one room and after some quiet discussions among the girls, Charlotte was fine taking a room with me, which I can't lie was quite exciting on my side. We went out on the first day to move around the river and I took several pictures as the girls posed around and had fun, since this was more like their get-together trip since college. They were catching up and enjoying every moment and I was right in the centre of it all. Charlotte beguiled me with her good looks and most of the photos I took were of her, of course; my lens could not stand being subjective at this point. Her friends didn't give me space to fully lay my intentions on the table for her, but I was looking for any chance me being around so that I could pour my heart out. I was ready to risk it all because beauty and curviness don't stay on market for long. One of her friends was a total dingus as she always sabotaged my charm with her belittling talks that were getting on my nerves, but the best way to keep it calm knowing that at the end of the day, Charlotte and I were to share a room.

It was a beautiful first day in terms of what the girls wanted to do and later in the night, we dined at a restaurant before going to the hotel. When we got to our room, it was exhaustion for everyone as it had been a long day, Charlotte went to the other room and joined the friends for a shower and when she returned, I was already on my bed with my laptop ready to watch a movie. This was my chance to say what I wanted to say and my first question to her as she sat on top of her bed was, "Are you single?" She rolled her eyes right back to me and replied, "I don't know." That was quite an open answer, and I was eager to know what that meant but she tried to put it that she had been with a guy, although she never took it seriously as there was less going on between them. That was enough for me to build on, because if a woman is not available, she will say she is not, but this was a call to try my luck and I was geared for that. Much as we didn't share much in high school times, Charlotte had always been open to a conversation with me and she was close to a friend, but this time I was seeing her in another aspect since we were all grown and she looked nothing like how she was back then. She was just stunning. She had on pump jeans that night and a light vest, and I jokingly commented on the jeans, "Will you be free in those jeans while sleeping?" It was a poking question, but she was very comfortable with her choice of night garment and she answered back with content, "I'm perfect." When she put off the light, I asked her if she was okay watching a movie with me and she was perfectly fine, after a long deliberation on what to watch, we settled for *The Escort*. This was a romance movie which an interesting storyline that captivated both of us, the laptop was at the edge of my bed, and it is at that point I requested Charlotte to come over to my bed so that she could get a clear view and be get comfortable. Fortunately, she was quick to agree, and she strolled across the room to my side of the bed and sat at the edge with her feet raised on top of the bed.

As she sat on my bed most of the time, I was distracted by the zesty perfume that she wore on her body, it was so calming that I wanted to hold her tight at this moment. We were at some moments turning to each other and having light conversations until the moment when I asked Charlotte if she wasn't feeling cold in her spot. She was hesitant with her reply but before even she said anything I offered to hold her in my arms through the movie time, which after a few thoughts she was happy about. She came close on my end and with my back rested on the headboard and legs stretched forward, I spread my left arm and she came close and put her head onto my chest. That was an inveigle moment for me with a romance movie playing and having a trophy of gold right in my arms, I just wanted the moment to go on longer. When Charlotte got into that position, we didn't move an inch throughout the movie but only got closer to each other and there were no signs of letting go. The movie ended, and it was already around 1 pm and we just didn't have to sleep. I didn't remove my hand from her and neither did she show signs of getting back to her bed. We stayed close to each other and talked about all kinds of things including sexual fantasies. Charlotte had a fantasy of making love in a forest, which was some weird thing to me, to be honest, and my fantasy was a simple one, making love in a bathtub. We laughed about it all but the best and most we got out of this moment was it drew us closer to each other emotionally and I was feeling a rash going over my body, which was always a sign of my emotional eruption. I was getting to put Charlotte in the chambers of my heart that had been blocked by sadness and deceit, she was becoming a key that unlocks all doors and whenever she presented me with a smile, it was enough for me to get the zeal to do anything; even if I was asked to encounter a snake, I would gladly do so even when those crawling things are my worst creatures. In the night Charlotte stayed by my side and we both lay straight on the bed as she was still resting on my chest. As we went deep into the night words sustained us and I remember pulling my hand away and letting her head sleep on the pillow while facing me. It was at that point that I could not resist the fire that was destined to burn me, I put my right hand around her neck and got close to her and pressed my lips on top of hers very calmly, I did the on-and-off kissing on top of her lips as if I was pulling a light switch and I was loving every moment of it. After those kisses, she kissed me back softly and I could feel her hand getting to my waist and holding me with a grip, her lips were so warm, soft, moist and sweet as honey, and our bodies fused heatedly. Our breath got heavy as our lips kept on exchanging with each other, and the rest of the world blurred around us, my body was limp, and I was unsure what end was up with us and as we were into it, Charlotte stopped and raised herself above my body, and she sat on top of me with her legs around my waist. She lowered down and continued to kiss me as she raised to look straight into my eyes. I was in an ineffable feeling. In that position at one moment, she held my hands and joined them above my head as she continued kissing me as though I was being put in cuffs. That truly gave me a kinky side of her but after sharing the longest kiss I had ever had, we didn't continue further from there and we cooled off, with her going back to her bed. I felt teased but at the same time I didn't feel ready to go further just as she also didn't get to it, so we both wished each other goodnight and tried to survive through the night of emotional spillage, which was hard, but we made it to morning.

We got to our last day of the trip and the girls had the most out of it as they tried to be engaged in different activities like quad biking, which I was also interested in, much as the quads were available for each one to ride. I didn't hesitate from requesting Charlotte to get on my back and we went around the field as she was holding me with her arms around my waist. Have you ever crossed paths with a person, and they ended up surprising you? This was one of those times because Charlotte was not a girl I had given much attention to. I was never attracted to her from those days of high school but each minute I spent with her was proving me wrong. She was once average to me, but she quickly became that precious gem of a diamond and in my eyes right now she was the most gorgeous person I knew, whenever my eyes landed on her I smiled because it was funny looking back. I was falling deep for her tiniest details like how she quarrelled with her friends, how she ate her food, how she held my waist on that quad bike or even how she glanced at me gently as if she was reminding me of how gentle last night was. I was falling for everything. There is a saying that "love always captures you; you never fall in love on your own. Love comes into your life when you least expect it, and it leaves when you most need it." This time love had found me and it seemed like my heart was not ready to give up on getting overwhelming feelings towards other people, it was another chance to feel, and it all seemed to like how you go out in a shop and buy a new item or gadget that you treasure immensely, and you hold it tight. Every time I looked at Charlotte throughout the day, it was a call to duty by my heart, it was ready to serve, and the body was up to the task, much as I thought of going slow and dropping whatever I felt, it didn't work because my feelings had already betrayed me. I was so convinced what I was feeling was not random but rather fate was doing what it does best, fixing the puzzle, it was a day of thoughts, fun and heart-fixing.

It got to the evening and the girls were tired, much as I was tired from taking their photos, and as we sat in the gardens of the hotel, I requested Charlotte for a walk, and she was happy to come around. I wanted to use this time to talk about last night and perhaps connect more, all I wanted was time with her and we moved away from the rest slowly and as we got to the bend where the friends could not see us, I reached out for her hand and held it in mine and trekked through pine trees. I told her of how my mind had been filled with thoughts of the moment we shared last night; she seemed fired up in her face and to my comfort, she told me she had been thinking about us. We got to sit under a shade and as we faced each other I told her of how she had awakened the dead cells in my heart, something she found amusing, but I was so serious with a straight face. I was ready for us to try out something so that we could know where we'd land. Her charming character made me want to explore more of her, she was the type that you would bet on. She had all qualities that are outstanding, very intelligent, modest and gentle, at times I was so delicate, thinking she might break. As we sat there, we talked of what each one wanted for a relationship, and I remember she was so straight to telling me that she just needed someone to connect with on an emotional level and someone who could be her support system in all aspects. I was ready for all that because what I felt for her right then was enough to make me what she wanted, I stretched more on having someone who was caring and patient with me. I just knew I was a broken soul in terms of knowing what I wanted exactly, but the one thing I never doubted was how my feelings for her were enough to fill a lake. She sat there looking at me speak and she told me something that made the day beautiful, she told me how she found me a handsome, interesting person. Some people give you compliments, and you question if they mean it or not, on this occasion I didn't question, I was just smiling so wide with fulfilment. That side conversation was a bonding moment that made us look at each other differently, it was at that moment we got attracted to each other more. We held each other's hands tight and walked around the block and when reaching the others, we let go as we were not ready to explain ourselves to a bunch that would make a series out of all this. We sat at the table, and we all ordered dinner. It was an evening worth reliving as it was filled with momentous times. Charlotte sat across the table and as I ate my eyes always escaped and landed on her cute face, which would always return indicators of love to me, I think we were blushing. Dinner ended and as we went back to the rooms, the girls came up with another plan, they wanted to go to the nightclub. I was exhausted by now and all I needed was a bed to lay on but when Charlotte jumped onto the wagon, that was it for me, I was ready to go and fetch that pleasure.

Everyone had to get ready, and the ladies took all their time to put themselves together. By the time they were all set to move out it was 10 pm, the rest of the girls put on tops and pant jeans but when Charlotte came out, she had on a short dress all hanging onto her body and was bringing out her curvy shape perfectly, something that weakened my knees because she was just pulchritudinous. I could not stop staring at this beautiful creature and my tongue could not keep it down, I told her she looked glamorous in that dress and was ready to hold her hand for stability as she wore stilettos to compliment the dress. We got a taxi to the nightclub, it was a popular place in the local area, and it had lots of tourists in place, we mingled in easily and the party was right made for us. I was a bit tired, and my mood was still catching up, but whenever I looked at Charlotte, my heartbeat suggested I was ready for the night. We didn't have drinkers in the group and the only things on the receipt were water and energy drinks. We secured a table with our drinks on top and for the first hour, we just recharged and cheered those who were on the dance floor. The funny thing about clubs is that if you can't dance at least you end up being the cheerleader of those on the floor. Music was loud and the mood was building, the girls started shaking from the chairs until they couldn't anymore. They moved to the centre of the dance floor and for me, the sight of the girls on the dance floor gave me a rush of happiness. I could not let the moment by and so I lifted my body with resolve to bring out all the dance strokes that I know. I'm a terrible dancer but the one thing you can't go wrong about is imitation, I did that all through and I was more like a programmed robot repeating exactly what other people were doing, but it was so fun. I got to dance with all the girls to different songs and the energy was high. I was astonished at how Charlotte moved her body in those spike heels. It got to the time when I got to find myself right in front of her and the song just got us at the moment where we just had to get hold of each other and move our bodies in a synchronising way to the music. She put her arms around my neck and my hands rested in her waist and our bodies didn't have an inch apart. I can't remember the song they were playing, but whichever it was, we slowed it down and just held on to each other with slight movements, we were feeling each other internally and it was as though my heart was being massaged at this moment. Like they say, if walls could talk, this time the dance floor would tell a story of energised spirits. The night was turning out to be the best for goodbyes as everyone was enjoying the bits off and I was full of desire for Charlotte as by this time I was very sure of what my heart was feeling. Charlotte and I got time off the dance floor and went back to the table and tried to just relax for the moment, we believe we both were seeing it in each other's eyes that we just wanted to go back to our room and have the moment to ourselves. From that tight dance, I was hard right now and had suffered the effects of blue balls from the previous night. Charlotte's candour was a big factor in my connection with her as she always put her heart out for you to see and she made it look like there was nothing to hide or not to give.

We went on with the outing until around 3 am when we thought that was enough of the fun we could have, we walked out of the club and fatigue was obvious with how we dragged our bodies, but when we went into the car, the drive was so quick that in no minute we were back at the hotel. The four girls said goodnight to us or rather a good morning and paced past our room quickly, all in need to rest their bodies. Charlotte and I were the last one to move from the hallway into our room and immediately as that door closed, we turned to each other and hugged so tightly, it was more like we all wanted the same thing at the right time. From that long hug Charlotte raised her head from my shoulder and kissed me on the lips slightly and she went away to access the bathroom. This time she was freer than the first night. She went into the shower and turned on the hot water and all I saw from the outside was her dress flying from the top and landing on the floor. She was naked for sure, and my mind was already figuring it out. The water ran for the next five minutes, and I heard Charlotte telling me, "If you want to shower you can join me or wait till I'm done." I was like no, I'm ready to join. I slid off my pants and top t-shirt so quickly that I think it was the quickest I have ever accomplished a task, I opened the shower door unsurely but when she turned around her eyes met mine with pure determination. I was very much naked, and Charlotte was right there with her body wet. It was hot inside and our bodies like this were a big turn-on. I felt powerless and my rod was already stretched out because Charlotte's body when hit with water was the most alluring and salacious body I had seen. It was calling out to me, and I went straight to her with her hands ready to grab me. I stood filled with a strong urge and in no second we were into each other kissing so fondly with libido, we just wanted each other and we were rubbing onto each other's body at this moment. The shower tap faced us, pouring the water on both our bodies around the chest and her boobs as it all dripped down to our feet, this all made us want to be into each other already. As I kissed her, as we were in that posture standing, I moved my hand down between her thighs and put my fingers around her juicy drawer. It was wet and slippery and as I kept feeling it, Charlotte was struggling to catch her breath and my bulge was strained with veins pumping through the skin. I could not wait another minute. I put Charlotte's back on the wall while standing and positioned her body facing me while lifting her left leg to brace against my waist area, I then entered, separating through her pink pearl with my hot beef injection. It was so warm and tight, and my thrusts upwards came in slowly but deep and kept on changing angles so that she could feel that manhood rubbing on her walls with pleasure. I was in the right position to push it in and out as my lips moved between Charlotte's lips and down to her chaste breasts, and it was how her moans kept me aroused that kept me steady in that slippery bathroom. As I was being turned into a miner, I thought getting to the floor would be the pinnacle of it all. I gently let Charlotte's leg down and held her hand to the centre of the bathroom and I sat down on the shower floor with my hands behind and my legs bent forward and Charlotte came between my legs in front of me and whizzed her hips until she sat on top of my bulge. My hands were behind, propping and pushing up her body with both of us facing in front as she did most of the riding. She kept her body moving in a circular grinding and I could feel my rod touch her deep to her walls. She was enjoying the moving of her body and I was as hard as she went on until the pleasure was intense, I just grabbed her waist from behind, trying to make her movement go faster until we both got to the time of release and excitement. We held each other so tight with both our bodies getting a shiver and after collecting our energies we finished the shower and retired to bed. Having Charlotte in my chest at that gave me total satisfaction and I felt accomplished.

We slept in the morning, but we had the longest sleep as our bed was surrounded with comfort and our minds were filled with peace, especially from knowing that we got each other all through. We woke up during the day and we were in a state of tranquillity with our faces always bearing broad grins, the girls seemed knocked out with fatigue and everyone was ready to go home. Some people are solivagants but by the look of things these girls had got the best from travelling as a group. I'm a complete ecophobia maniac who enjoys every chance of being away from home and this time on this trip every second paid off, especially since I got to have Charlotte in my personal space. That was the true definition of my trip with the girls. Travelling gets us to places where special things can happen and everlasting memories are made, and that is why I normally can't stay in one place, my feet get to itch and just like Rachel Wolchin said, "If we were meant to stay in one place, we'd have roots instead of feet." However, nothing lasts forever and on that note, we got back to town and everyone had to go back to their place of residence. I stayed with several photos, which I worked on the following days. They were beautiful pictures, but the fun part was me getting to have Charlotte's photos without sending that awkward WhatsApp message stating, "some pictures". I gave the girls their well-edited pictures and they paid half the money for my services since I equally enjoyed the trip, and everyone was happy at the end of the day. I kept Charlotte close in my life and I was not planning to distance myself at any moment because knowing that she was my life gave me a sense of serenity. She was a town girl who lived in the centre of the capital city, whereas I was from the suburbs, but that came with merit since I always got to see her when I was in town and we would go for pizza Tuesdays every week. Most of our argument on these dates was about her eating pizza with pineapple or better known as Hawaiian pizza. That made me ache because that was a wrong preference for me but after a few times of keeping her around me she made me love it and to this day I'm the greatest defender of Hawaiian pizza. Our conversations were very pure and came easily, she was full of eunoia, and the comicality of her personality always stood out because she always made me burst out laughing. We appeared compatible and that was making everything easy. We would sometimes just go for walks in the park holding hands and swinging them like primary school kids and the excitement was always there in our eyes. She made everything have sense and her future was so clear that there was no way she said a thing and I was sidelined or not the centre of it. She gave me the importance of line which made me realise my purpose in life. She was my strong woman and we had made this a strong relationship built on honesty and trust. When I was not with her it was vital to me to at least send her a message every hour. That way I was keeping present in her life, and she was always happy to hear from me. She made our relationship querencia and every day was a new day for me to be in love. What I was having with Charlotte at this level is something I can't express, since love is a sensation that can't be expressed in words. What we shared was on foundations of respect for each other and we both understood the commitment that we were making to each other. I can't deny that as we went on with us being in a loop of affection, it was scary, providing someone access to a list of all your faults and imperfections and trusting them to use their influence responsibly, it's a bet but when done, it is the most beautiful thing a human can do, being vulnerable. I always looked forward to her kisses. Whenever she approached me in that sense, she would put her warm lips on mine so gently and our tongues would tangle and go to war as we battled for dominance within our closed mouths. That always made me want to lift her up and just rip her clothes apart in passion with the urge of both of us getting total satisfaction.

I was with Charlotte for almost a year now and we were almost in each other's daily aspects. She had got to know where I stayed as she had made the effort to at least come to visit on several occasions and my elder brother, whom I was staying with most of the times, had gotten to know of her and how we were in a serious relationship. My brother always wanted to be the wise one with all sorts of advice but I was not ready to listen to a bit of it because he was a failure in holding a relationship. So if you fail at something, what makes you think that you're the best person to talk about it? A Monday is a day when everyone gets out to start the week with zeal at their jobs or work and that was no different to my brother. Me being a freelancer who spent most of the time indoors or in places, a week started and I had nothing going on with me and I could not think beyond wanting to spend some time with a woman who had wrapped my heart into her palms. I called Charlotte that morning and coincidentally she was free, I asked her to come around if it was okay with her and she was more than ready because she also treasured being around me. I tried to clean the house just not to embarrass myself with my disorganisation, and since my bedroom had two-decker beds, it was never the ideal place for me and Charlotte. I arranged and organised my brother's bedroom as it was better with a double bed. When it got to 2 pm, Charlotte showed up in an Uber and I went out of the house to welcome her with a big embrace of a hug. She kissed me on my cheek, and we went into the house. We sat in the sitting room, and she pulled out chocolate muffins. Those were our favourites to eat together because I believed it was always our sign of love, they were so sweet, and we always had a signature of each one feeding the other at least once. I think it's important to always have small things that you do together that you hold on to. Those things are the memories you hold on to fondly. It was an afternoon of us being close to each other and watching movies, which was a hobby for both of us. Later, Charlotte said she wanted to rest for a bit and the only place I had prepared perfectly enough was my brother's room. I held her by the hand and took her to the room and she lay on top of the bed gently on her abdomen, I left the room and went back to the sitting room for a few minutes and then I could not settle in my seat. I went back to the room and asked Charlotte if I could lay beside her, she agreed and I lay next to her, she had turned on her right arm and I slept looking in the same direction with my arm wrapped around her waist and the other raised above my head. We spent some time in quiet and it was beautiful how we were just not saying anything at that moment yet saying too much. After all that Charlotte said in her calm voice, "I love you." It was at this moment that I first thought of marriage, I was so in love that all my future was starting to make perfect sense with her in it. She had stroked the fibres in my body that had not seen what real affection was. I was in love, and I told her proudly how I felt, it was powerful but most significantly bonding. She turned around and faced me, her eyes were teary, and her lips were slightly open. We had become broken by emotions and feelings that are far greater than our imaginations. She put her fingers on my lips as she looked on and started moving her fingers all around my facial features as if she was asking herself what she could do for me. She pushed her body and tagged it to mine and put her sugary lips on mine, kissing me, her lips were still sweet with the muffin cake we had just eaten not long ago. Charlotte's torso began to warm up, and sparks started to fly as I leaned in close and carefully brushed our lips together more. My tummy started to flutter as I inhaled her perfume and the gentle peachy fragrance of her conditioner. However, Charlotte was overcome with tenderness as she leaned in for the kiss, my lips being incredibly gentle against hers.

We were overwhelmed by the fire within our bodies, I shifted my body and went on top of her body with a strong longing for union. I slowly flipped the t-shirt she had on and I put it off over her head, in turn I removed mine, leaned back down and went for more of her mushy lips. I started making my way down as I put my lips around her neck, down to her bra, which I unclipped so quickly as if as aiming for treasure, those titties were well-endowed and my lips fit perfect on those sharp nipples, I sucked them putting my tongue over them and Charlotte put her hand tightly on my shoulder with her lips apart for heavy breaths. I didn't last long before my tongue got to the naval area, which she enjoyed feeling my tongue go round it. I got to her waist, and it was then that I put my hands on her long skirt that she had on and slid it off and took off the inner covering, I spread her legs apart and took off my shorts slowly before I buried my head between her thighs. She screamed with pleasure at her seabed being massaged by my tongue in a stroking circular movement and in no minute I was back up with her legs around my waist and I tenderly straightened my phallus and slid it down into her mossy cleft. This was the gentlest we had ever been and we were locked into eye contact as my thrusts went through her slit in and out in a circular motion, we were sweaty and hot and the only part moving on me was my waist area and us exchanging kisses intermittently. We held so tight, and I could feel her legs cling around my waist and her hands firm on my back, I felt dipped in an ocean filled with love and as my bulge enlarged within her I was intensifying my penetration as I wished to make love to her until she was too exhausted to move an inch from the bed and until she called me in her dreams. Our lower parts were soaked with pleasure and dripping filled my thighs until our climax point. The intensity of that moment made us not doubt each other as we lay on that bed naked. Time had shifted and I had to make sure my brother didn't find us all dolled up on his bed, Charlotte was indeed exhausted and so was I, but we had energy left in us to get ourselves together. We order an Uber and we went together up to her home and then I found my way back home.

I was in a beautiful, committed relationship and I was so sure of us having mutual feelings, we made communication our biggest weapon and trust was supplementing everything in this relationship. I had to think about how to work more and put foundations that would benefit us. Deep down I knew I would ask Charlotte for marriage if things kept the way they were, but money was always part of it. Offers were going around of going into the diaspora where we could do certain jobs and earn good money. It was an exciting offer and so I sat down with Charlotte and told her of my intentions. I wanted to give it a try and see if it came with some positive change. She was positive about it, and she turned out supportive. I sent in my request and applied, but within a short time the company was already exchanging emails and like that, I was to travel and work from abroad on a two-year contract. It was a hard time for me and Charlotte, but we had settled for this and braced for a long-distance relationship. On my departure day, she was there beside me at the airport and exchanged kisses and hugs like we never wanted to be apart at any minute, but it was time.

I left the country not the happiest man, but I had hope that I would return home any time and hold my love again in my arms. I reached my destination country, and I embarked on a journey of hard work, the job I got was working as a porter in a kitchen equipment company and all we did was deliver different equipment to customers around the country. It was hard when it came to moving heavy big equipment, I never loved that bit, and after a long day you lay down on your bed and get to think of the one you love. The distance was a pain that I could not get rid of but the long conversations at night and messages during the day comforted me all through. Time stalled during work hours, but it was in no minute I was almost making her abroad and it was Charlotte's birthday. It was sad that I was not going to be there for her birthday, but I made sure she had a good day. I got contacts and made her a cake, which was delivered, and sent some money for her to have the best time. Since I was left with ten months of staying abroad, I was so sure that I was to go back and enjoy myself with her more, we didn't talk much on the day and after work, we exchanged a few messages, although I noticed I could not see her profile picture and status on WhatsApp. This filled my heart with doubt and scepticism and just like that I contacted a mutual friend and told her to send me Charlotte's profile picture and status since my phone had issues, to my surprise she did send through a picture and a screenshot of a status. I was flabbergasted by what I saw in the picture: it was Charlotte feeding a piece of cake to a guy and in the status, it was reading, "thank you very much babe for making my day special." I felt weak at that moment and sadness filled my heart because that was perfidiousness. All I did was send the picture to her and cropped the status and sent it too, and I followed it with "thank you". She instantly called but I didn't pick up and the best I had to do was get in bed and sleep because my heart was aching and the body was trembling. I just couldn't fathom what I experienced.

The following day I woke up and went to work but my strength was tested all through. I was still putting myself together. Later that day I decided to hear what Charlotte had to say but when we got to the topic she had a lot of hesitance and the best story she came up with was that her sisters had put her to it. They got her the guy whom she had just started talking to and it was on her birthday she got to see him, she insisted it was nothing. Of course, I didn't believe a thing about what she explained, and my trust was completely shattered from there, although I fronted equanimity. I tried to push on with her, but things were not the same. When I made one year, it was my time for vacation and so I arranged to go spend a month just to have fun and see my family, Charlotte was still a big part of my life even though I was pushed back with disloyalty. I still carried love for her. I travelled and reached home, and family was there to welcome me and take me through my stay, as for Charlotte, I didn't see her immediately. I was laid back and I was not sure if I could trust her and go on with everything as though it was normal. However, in the third week of my vacation, I met with Charlotte in a hotel one evening and she tried to explain everything, but she could not exhaust why she had blocked me from seeing her profile or status. Our differences didn't keep us apart, however, when it came to night-time. Charlotte sat me on a chair in the hotel and undressed me fully with control and she used my belt and tied my hands from behind, I was just there naked and powerless with a hard-on. She undressed off her clothes swiftly and started kissing my body parts from head to toe, and then she put her legs around my waist and just sat on my rod. She was in control of the pace and the riding was all for her to take as all I was feeling was her wet slit dripping to my balls. I loved her kinky side of things. She took it all until she was done with me and then untied my hands. I can't deny I still think of that sex. We slept together that night and, in the morning, we went our separate ways. The time reached when my vacation was over and this time I went to town and said goodbye to her from our favourite pizza spot, we both still had a love for each other although I was not sure if I trusted her anymore.

I left the country and went back to my hustle which I was getting good at because one year was long enough for me to adjust. I kept on communicating with Charlotte, although the intensity and frequency had changed. After three weeks when I was back from my vacation, I last heard from Charlotte two days before. The day was bright and hot, which kept my mood low for part of the day. I never got to have direct calls from my native country but this time I got a weird call, I had a feeling that I shouldn't pick but I ended up picking and I had a shaky voice speak. "Charlotte is dead." I got a sound in my ears that was so loud, and my breathing got fast, my body instantly turned cold, and I was shaking uncontrollably, the news was a physical blow to my body as I could not believe what I had just heard. This pushed me into total misery, but the worst part was that Charlotte had lost her life while carrying out an abortion. I was puzzled because I didn't know about her being pregnant. I was asking many questions and the best person who would be there with answers was gone, I was never going to hold her in my arms and all I had built in my heart for her came crashing down. I was heartbroken and up to now I don't know if the pregnancy she had was mine or someone else. Why wouldn't she tell me? I believe Charlotte was the aftermath of all my past experiences, she made me want to stay and fight on building an empire together, we had connected to a level that surpassed everything, and with this grief, I've discovered that it is all love, it's all the affection you want but are unable to offer. In the corners of your eyes, all that misplaced affection accumulates, feeling the neck tumour, and the area of your ribcage that is empty. Grief is simply affection without a destination. Even when I carry Charlotte every day of my life, and I wish she was here to talk to me because I feel she left me with a lot of questions, I am not about to give up on love. Just as Maya Angelou said, "Have enough courage to trust love one more time and always one more time." The adventure of my heart is just at the base with a slope, ridge and face to manoeuvre before I get to the peak.